William Butler Yeats, Jack Butler Yeats

Irish fairy tales

William Butler Yeats, Jack Butler Yeats

Irish fairy tales

ISBN/EAN: 9783744729529

Printed in Europe, USA, Canada, Australia, Japan

Cover: Foto ©Andreas Hilbeck / pixelio.de

More available books at **www.hansebooks.com**

THE CHILDREN'S
LIBRARY

IRISH FAIRY TALES

THE CHILDREN'S LIBRARY.

THE BROWN OWL.

A CHINA CUP, AND OTHER STORIES.

STORIES FROM FAIRYLAND.

THE LITTLE PRINCESS.

THE STORY OF A PUPPET.

TALES FROM THE MABINOGION.

IRISH FAIRY TALES.

(*Others in the Press.*)

"PLAYING AWAY ON THE PIPES AS MERRILY AS IF
NOTHING HAD HAPPENED."   [*Page* 48.

IRISH
FAIRY TALES

EDITED

WITH AN INTRODUCTION

BY

W. B. YEATS

AUTHOR OF 'THE WANDERINGS OF OISIN,' ETC.

ILLUSTRATED BY JACK B. YEATS

LONDON
T. FISHER UNWIN
1892

WHERE MY BOOKS GO.

All the words that I gather,
   And all the words that I write,
Must spread out their wings untiring,
   And never rest in their flight,
Till they come where your sad, sad
      heart is,
   And sing to you in the night,
Beyond where the waters are moving,
   Storm darkened or starry bright.

                  W. B. YEATS.

LONDON, *January 1892.*

CONTENTS

PAGE

INTRODUCTION . . . 1

LAND AND WATER FAIRIES

THE FAIRIES' DANCING-PLACE . 13

THE RIVAL KEMPERS . . . 17

THE YOUNG PIPER . . . 32

A FAIRY ENCHANTMENT . . 49

TEIGUE OF THE LEE . . . 53

THE FAIRY GREYHOUND . . 69

THE LADY OF GOLLERUS . . 77

EVIL SPIRITS

PAGE

THE DEVIL'S MILL . . . 95

FERGUS O'MARA AND THE AIR-
DEMONS 112

THE MAN WHO NEVER KNEW FEAR . 123

CATS

SEANCHAN THE BARD AND THE KING
OF THE CATS . . . 141

OWNEY AND OWNEY-NA-PEAK . 151

KINGS AND WARRIORS

THE KNIGHTING OF CUCULAIN . 185

THE LITTLE WEAVER OF DULEEK
GATE 195

APPENDIX

CLASSIFICATION OF IRISH FAIRIES . 223

AUTHORITIES ON IRISH FOLKLORE . 234

INTRODUCTION

AN IRISH STORY-TELLER

I AM often doubted when I say that the Irish peasantry still believe in fairies. People think I am merely trying to bring back a little of the old dead beautiful world of romance into this century of great engines and spinning-jinnies. Surely the hum of wheels and clatter of printing presses, to let alone the lecturers with their black coats and tumblers of water, have driven away the goblin kingdom and made silent the feet of the little dancers.

Old Biddy Hart at any rate does not think so. Our bran-new opinions have never been heard of under her brown-thatched roof tufted with yellow stone-crop. It is not so long since I sat by the turf fire eating her griddle cake in her cottage on the slope of Benbulben and asking after her friends, the fairies, who inhabit the green thorn-covered hill up there behind her house. How firmly she believed in them! how greatly she feared offending them! For a long time she would give me no answer but 'I always mind my own affairs and they always mind theirs.' A little talk about my great-grandfather who lived all his life in the valley below, and a few words to remind her how I myself was often under her roof when but seven or eight years old loosened her tongue, however. It would be less dangerous at any rate to talk to me of the fairies than it would be to tell some 'Towrow' of them, as she contemptuously called English tourists, for I had lived under the shadow of their own hillsides. She did not forget, however, to remind me to say after we had finished, 'God bless them, Thursday' (that being the day), and so ward off their displeasure, in case they were angry at our notice, for they love to live and dance unknown of men.

Once started, she talked on freely enough, her face glowing in the firelight as she bent over the griddle or stirred the turf, and told how such a one was stolen away from near Coloney village and made to live seven years among 'the gentry,' as she calls the fairies for politeness' sake, and how when she came home she had no toes, for she had danced them off; and how such another was taken from the neighbouring village of Grange and compelled to nurse the child of the queen of the fairies a few months before I came. Her news about the creatures is always quite matter-of-fact and detailed, just as if she dealt with any common occur-

rence : the late fair, or the dance at
Rosses last year, when a bottle of whisky
was given to the best man, and a cake
tied up in ribbons to the best woman
dancer.   They are, to her, people not so
different from herself, only grander and
finer in every way.   They have the most
beautiful parlours and drawing-rooms,
she would tell you, as an old man told
me once.   She has endowed them with
all she knows of splendour, although
that is not such a great deal, for her
imagination is easily pleased.   What
does not seem to us so very wonderful
is wonderful to her, there, where all is
so homely under her wood rafters and
her thatched ceiling covered with white-
washed canvas.   We have pictures and
books to help us imagine a splendid
fairy world of gold and silver, of
crowns and marvellous draperies ; but
she has only that little picture of St.
Patrick over the fireplace, the bright-
coloured crockery on the dresser, and
the sheet of ballads stuffed by her

young daughter behind the stone dog on the mantelpiece. Is it strange, then, if her fairies have not the fantastic glories of the fairies you and I are wont to see in picture-books and read of in stories? She will tell you of peasants who met the fairy cavalcade and thought it but a troop of peasants like themselves until it vanished into shadow and night, and of great fairy palaces that were mistaken, until they melted away, for the country seats of rich gentlemen.

Her views of heaven itself have the same homeliness, and she would be quite as naïve about its personages if the chance offered as was the pious Clondalkin laundress who told a friend of mine that she had seen a vision of St. Joseph, and that he had 'a lovely shining hat upon him and a shirt-buzzom that was never starched in this world.' She would have mixed some quaint poetry with it, however; for there is a world of difference

between Benbulben and Dublinised
Clondalkin.

Heaven and Fairyland—to these has
Biddy Hart given all she dreams of
magnificence, and to them her soul
goes out—to the one in love and
hope, to the other in love and fear—
day after day and season after season ;
saints and angels, fairies and witches,
haunted thorn-trees and holy wells, are
to her what books, and plays, and
pictures are to you and me. Indeed
they are far more ; for too many among
us grow prosaic and commonplace, but
she keeps ever a heart full of music.
'I stand here in the doorway,' she said
once to me on a fine day, 'and look at
the mountain and think of the good-
ness of God'; and when she talks of
the fairies I have noticed a touch of
tenderness in her voice. She loves
them because they are always young,
always making festival, always far off
from the old age that is coming upon
her and filling her bones with aches,

and because, too, they are so like little children.

Do you think the Irish peasant would be so full of poetry if he had not his fairies? Do you think the peasant girls of Donegal, when they are going to service inland, would kneel down as they do and kiss the sea with their lips if both sea and land were not made lovable to them by beautiful legends and wild sad stories? Do you think the old men would take life so cheerily and mutter their proverb, 'The lake is not burdened by its swan, the steed by its bridle, or a man by the soul that is in him,' if the multitude of spirits were not near them?

W. B. YEATS.

CLONDALKIN,
July 1891.

NOTE

I HAVE to thank Lady Wilde for leave to give 'Seanchan the Bard' from her *Ancient Legends of Ireland* (Ward and Downey), the most poetical and ample collection of Irish folk-lore yet published; Mr. Standish O'Grady for leave to give 'The Knighting of Cuculain' from that prose epic he has curiously named *History of Ireland, Heroic Period*; Professor Joyce for his 'Fergus O'Mara and the Air Demons'; and Mr. Douglas Hyde for his unpublished story, 'The Man who never knew Fear.'

I have included no story that has already appeared in my *Fairy and Folk Tales of the Irish Peasantry* (Camelot Series).

The two volumes make, I believe, a fairly representative collection of Irish folk tales.

LAND AND WATER
FAIRIES

THE FAIRIES' DANCING-PLACE

By William Carleton

LANTY M'CLUSKY had married a wife, and, of course, it was necessary to have a house in which to keep her. Now, Lanty had taken a bit of a farm, about six acres; but as there was no house on it, he resolved to build one; and that it might be as comfortable as possible, he selected for the site of it one of those beautiful green circles that are supposed to be the play-ground of the fairies. Lanty was warned against this; but

as he was a headstrong man, and not
much given to fear, he said he would
not change such a pleasant situation
for his house to oblige all the fairies
in Europe.   He accordingly proceeded
with the building, which he finished
off very neatly ; and, as it is usual on
these occasions to give one's neighbours and friends a house-warming,
so, in compliance with this good and
pleasant old custom, Lanty having
brought home the wife in the course
of the day, got a fiddler and a lot of
whisky, and gave those who had come
to see him a dance in the evening.
This was all very well, and the fun
and hilarity were proceeding briskly,
when a noise was heard after night
had set in, like a crushing and strain-
ing of ribs and rafters on the top of
the house.   The folks assembled all
listened, and, without doubt, there
was nothing heard but crushing, and
heaving, and pushing, and groaning,
and panting, as if a thousand little

men were engaged in pulling down
the roof.

'Come,' said a voice which spoke
in a tone of command, 'work hard :
you know we must have Lanty's house
down before midnight.'

This was an unwelcome piece of
intelligence to Lanty, who, finding
that his enemies were such as he
could not cope with, walked out, and
addressed them as follows :

'Gintlemen, I humbly ax yer pardon
for buildin' on any place belongin' to
you ; but if you'll have the civilitude
to let me alone this night, I'll begin
to pull down and remove the house
to-morrow morning.'

This was followed by a noise like
the clapping of a thousand tiny little
hands, and a shout of 'Bravo, Lanty !
build half-way between the two White-
thorns above the boreen'; and after
another hearty little shout of exulta-
tion, there was a brisk rushing noise,
and they were heard no more.

The story, however, does not end here; for Lanty, when digging the foundation of his new house, found the full of a *kam*[1] of gold: so that in leaving to the fairies their playground, he became a richer man than ever he otherwise would have been, had he never come in contact with them at all.

[1] *Kam*—a metal vessel in which the peasantry dip rushlights.

THE RIVAL KEMPERS

By William Carleton

IN the north of Ireland there are spinning meetings of unmarried females frequently held at the houses of farmers, called *kemps*. Every young woman who has got the reputation of being a quick and expert spinner attends where the kemp is to be held, at an hour usually before daylight, and on these occasions she is accompanied by her sweetheart or some male relative, who carries her wheel, and conducts her safely across the fields or along the road, as the case may be. A kemp is, indeed, an animated and joyous scene, and one, besides, which is calculated to promote industry and decent pride. Scarcely anything can be more cheering and agreeable than to hear at a distance, breaking the silence of morning, the light-hearted voices of many girls either in mirth or song, the humming sound of the busy wheels—jarred upon a little, it is true, by the stridulous noise and checkings of the reels, and the voices of the reelers, as they call aloud the checks, together with the name of the girl and the quantity she has spun up to that period; for the contest is generally commenced two or three hours before daybreak. This mirthful spirit is also sustained by the prospect of a dance—with which, by the way, every kemp closes; and when the fair victor is declared, she is to be looked upon as the queen of the meeting, and treated with the necessary respect.

But to our tale. Every one knew

Shaun Buie M'Gaveran to be the cleanest, best-conducted boy, and the most industrious too, in the whole parish of Faugh-a-ballagh. Hard was it to find a young fellow who could handle a flail, spade, or reaping-hook in better style, or who could go through his day's work in a more creditable or workmanlike manner. In addition to this, he was a fine, well-built, handsome young man as you could meet in a fair; and so, sign was on it, maybe the pretty girls weren't likely to pull each other's caps about him. Shaun, however, was as prudent as he was good-looking; and although he wanted a wife, yet the sorrow one of him but preferred taking a well-handed, smart girl, who was known to be well-behaved and industrious, like himself. Here, however, was where the puzzle lay on him; for instead of one girl of that kind, there were in the neighbourhood no less than a dozen of them—all equally fit and willing to become his

wife, and all equally good-looking.
There were two, however, whom he
thought a trifle above the rest ; but so
nicely balanced were Biddy Corrigan
and Sally Gorman, that for the life of
him he could not make up his mind
to decide between them.   Each of
them had won her kemp ; and it was
currently said by them who ought to
know, that neither of them could over-
match the other.   No two girls in the
parish were better respected, or deserved
to be so ; and the consequence was,
they had every one's good word and
good wish.   Now it so happened that
Shaun had been pulling a cord with
each ; and as he knew not how to
decide between, he thought he would
allow them to do that themselves if
they could.   He accordingly gave out
to the neighbours that he would hold
a kemp on that day week, and he told
Biddy and Sally especially that he had
made up his mind to marry whichever
of them won the kemp, for he knew

right well, as did all the parish, that one of them must. The girls agreed to this very good-humouredly, Biddy telling Sally that she (Sally) would surely win it; and Sally, not to be outdone in civility, telling the same thing to her.

Well, the week was nearly past, there being but two days till that of the kemp, when, about three o'clock, there walks into the house of old Paddy Corrigan a little woman dressed in high-heeled shoes and a short red cloak. There was no one in the house but Biddy at the time, who rose up and placed a chair near the fire, and asked the little red woman to sit down and rest herself. She accordingly did so, and in a short time a lively chat commenced between them.

'So,' said the strange woman, 'there's to be a great kemp in Shaun Buie M'Gaveran's?'

'Indeed there is that, good woman,' replied Biddy, smiling and blushing to back of that again, because she knew her own fate depended on it.

'And,' continued the little woman, 'whoever wins the kemp wins a husband?'

'Ay, so it seems.'

'Well, whoever gets Shaun will be a happy woman, for he's the moral of a good boy.'

'That's nothing but the truth, anyhow,' replied Biddy, sighing, for fear, you may be sure, that she herself might lose him; and indeed a young woman might sigh from many a worse reason. 'But,' said she, changing the subject, 'you appear to be tired, honest woman, an' I think you had better eat a bit, an' take a good drink of *buinnhe ramwher* (thick milk) to help you on your journey.'

'Thank you kindly, a colleen,' said the woman; 'I'll take a bit, if you plase, hopin', at the same time, that you won't be the poorer of it this day twelve months,'

'Sure,' said the girl, 'you know

that what we give from kindness ever an' always leaves a blessing behind it.'

'Yes, acushla, when it *is* given from kindness.'

She accordingly helped herself to the food that Biddy placed before her, and appeared, after eating, to be very much refreshed.

'Now,' said she, rising up, 'you're a very good girl, an' if you are able to find out my name before Tuesday morning, the kemp-day, I tell you that you'll win it, and gain the husband.'

'Why,' said Biddy, 'I never saw you before. I don't know who you are, nor where you live; how then can I ever find out your name?'

'You never saw me before, sure enough,' said the old woman, 'an' I tell you that you never will see me again but once; an' yet if you have not my name for me at the close of the kemp, you'll lose all, an' that will leave you a sore heart, for well I know you love Shaun Buie.'

So saying, she went away, and left
poor Biddy quite cast down at what
she had said, for, to tell the truth, she
loved Shaun very much, and had no
hopes of being able to find out the
name of the little woman, on which,
it appeared, so much to her depended.

It was very near the same hour of
the same day that Sally Gorman was
sitting alone in her father's house,
thinking of the kemp, when who
should walk in to her but our friend
the little red woman.

'God save you, honest woman,' said
Sally, 'this is a fine day that's in it,
the Lord be praised!'

'It is,' said the woman, 'as fine
a day as one could wish for: indeed
it is.'

'Have you no news on your travels?'
asked Sally.

'The only news in the neighbourhood,' replied the other, 'is this great
kemp that's to take place at Shaun
Buie M'Gaveran's. They say you're

either to win him or lose him then,'
she added, looking closely at Sally as
she spoke.

'I'm not very much afraid of that,'
said Sally, with confidence; 'but even
if I do lose him, I may get as good.'

'It's not easy gettin' as good,'
rejoined the old woman, 'an' you
ought to be very glad to win him, if
you can.'

'Let me alone for that,' said Sally.
'Biddy's a good girl, I allow; but as
for spinnin', she never saw the day
she could leave me behind her. Won't
you sit an' rest you?' she added;
'maybe you're tired.'

'It's time for you to think of it,'
thought the woman, but she spoke
nothing: 'but,' she added to herself
on reflection, 'it's better late than
never—I'll sit awhile, till I see a little
closer what she's made of.'

She accordingly sat down and chatted
upon several subjects, such as young
women like to talk about, for about

half an hour; after which she arose,
and taking her little staff in hand, she
bade Sally good-bye, and went her
way. After passing a little from the
house she looked back, and could not
help speaking to herself as follows:

> ' She's smooth and smart,
>   But she wants the heart ;
> · She's tight and neat,
>   But she gave no meat.'

Poor Biddy now made all possible
inquiries about the old woman, but to
no purpose. Not a soul she spoke to
about her had ever seen or heard of
such a woman. She felt very dispirited,
and began to lose heart, for there is
no doubt that if she missed Shaun it
would have cost her many a sorrowful
day. She knew she would never get
his equal, or at least any one that she
loved so well. At last the kemp day
came, and with it all the pretty girls
of the neighbourhood to Shaun Buie's.
Among the rest, the two that were to

decide their right to him were doubtless the handsomest pair by far, and
every one admired them.   To be sure,
it was a blythe and merry place, and
many a light laugh and sweet song
rang out from pretty lips that day.
Biddy and Sally, as every one expected,
were far ahead of the rest, but so even
in their spinning that the reelers could
not for the life of them declare which
was the better.   It was neck-and-neck
and head-and-head between the pretty
creatures, and all who were at the
kemp felt themselves wound up to the
highest pitch of interest and curiosity
to know which of them would be
successful.

The day was now more than half
gone, and no difference was between
them, when, to the surprise and sorrow
of every one present, Biddy Corrigan's
heck broke in two, and so to all appearance ended the contest in favour of
her rival; and what added to her
mortification, she was as ignorant of

the red little woman's name as ever. What was to be done? All that could be done was done. Her brother, a boy of about fourteen years of age, happened to be present when the accident took place, having been sent by his father and mother to bring them word how the match went on between the rival spinsters. Johnny Corrigan was accordingly despatched with all speed to Donnel M'Cusker's, the wheelwright, in order to get the heck mended, that being Biddy's last but hopeless chance. Johnny's anxiety that his sister should win was of course very great, and in order to lose as little time as possible he struck across the country, passing through, or rather close by, Kilrudden forth, a place celebrated as a resort of the fairies. What was his astonishment, however, as he passed a white-thorn tree, to hear a female voice singing, in accompaniment to the sound of a spinning-wheel, the following words:

'There's a girl in this town doesn't know my
    name;
But my name's Even Trot—Even Trot.'

'There's a girl in this town,' said
the lad, 'who's in great distress, for
she has broken her heck, and lost a
husband. I'm now goin' to Donnel
M'Cusker's to get it mended.'

'What's her name?' said the little
red woman.

'Biddy Corrigan.'

The little woman immediately
whipped out the heck from her own
wheel, and giving it to the boy, desired
him to take it to his sister, and never
mind Donnel M'Cusker.

'You have little time to lose,' she
added, 'so go back and give her this;
but don't tell her how you got it, nor,
above all things, that it was Even Trot
that gave it to you.'

The lad returned, and after giving
the heck to his sister, as a matter of
course told her that it was a little red
woman called Even Trot that sent it

to her, a circumstance which made tears of delight start to Biddy's eyes, for she knew now that Even Trot was the name of the old woman, and having known that, she felt that something good would happen to her. She now resumed her spinning, and never did human fingers let down the thread so rapidly. The whole kemp were amazed at the quantity which from time to time filled her pirn. The hearts of her friends began to rise, and those of Sally's party to sink, as hour after hour she was fast approaching her rival, who now spun if possible with double speed on finding Biddy coming up with her. At length they were again even, and just at that moment in came her friend the little red woman, and asked aloud, 'Is there any one in this kemp that knows my name?' This question she asked three times before Biddy could pluck up courage to answer her. She at last said,

'There's a girl in this town does know your
   name—
Your name is Even Trot—Even Trot.'

   'Ay,' said the old woman, 'and so
it is ; and let that name be your guide
and your husband's through life.   Go
steadily along, but let your step be
even ; stop little ; keep always advanc-
ing ; and you'll never have cause to
rue the day that you first saw Even
Trot.'

   We need scarcely add that Biddy
won the kemp and the husband, and
that she and Shaun lived long and
happily together ; and I have only now
to wish, kind reader, that you and I
may live longer and more happily still.

THE YOUNG PIPER

By Crofton Croker

THERE lived not long since, on the borders of the county Tipperary, a decent honest couple, whose names were Mick Flannigan and Judy Muldoon. These poor people were blessed, as the saying is, with four children, all boys : three of them were as fine, stout, healthy, good-looking children as ever the sun shone upon ; and it was enough to make any Irishman proud of the breed of his countrymen to see them about one o'clock on a fine summer's day standing at their father's cabin

door, with their beautiful flaxen hair
hanging in curls about their head, and
their cheeks like two rosy apples, and
a big laughing potato smoking in their
hand.   A proud man was Mick of
these fine children, and a proud woman,
too, was Judy; and reason enough
they had to be so.   But it was far
otherwise with the remaining one,
which was the third eldest: he was
the most miserable, ugly, ill-conditioned
brat that ever God put life into; he
was so ill-thriven that he never was able
to stand alone, or to leave his cradle;
he had long, shaggy, matted, curled
hair, as black as the soot; his face
was of a greenish-yellow colour; his
eyes were like two burning coals, and
were for ever moving in his head, as if
they had the perpetual motion.   Before he was a twelvemonth old he had
a mouth full of great teeth; his hands
were like kites' claws, and his legs were
no thicker than the handle of a whip,
and about as straight as a reaping-

D

hook : to make the matter worse, he had the appetite of a cormorant, and the whinge, and the yelp, and the screech, and the yowl, was never out of his mouth.

The neighbours all suspected that he was something not right, particularly as it was observed, when people, as they do in the country, got about the fire, and began to talk of religion and good things, the brat, as he lay in the cradle, which his mother generally put near the fireplace that he might be snug, used to sit up, as they were in the middle of their talk, and begin to bellow as if the devil was in him in right earnest ; this, as I said, led the neighbours to think that all was not right, and there was a general consultation held one day about what would be best to do with him. Some advised to put him out on the shovel, but Judy's pride was up at that. A pretty thing indeed, that a child of hers should be put on a shovel and flung

out on the dunghill just like a dead
kitten or a poisoned rat; no, no, she
would not hear to that at all. One
old woman, who was considered very
skilful and knowing in fairy matters,
strongly recommended her to put the
tongs in the fire, and heat them red
hot, and to take his nose in them, and
that would beyond all manner of doubt
make him tell what he was and where
he came from (for the general suspicion
was, that he had been changed by the
good people); but Judy was too soft-
hearted, and too fond of the imp, so
she would not give in to this plan,
though everybody said she was wrong,
and maybe she was, but it's hard to
blame a mother. Well, some advised
one thing, and some another; at last
one spoke of sending for the priest,
who was a very holy and a very learned
man, to see it. To this Judy of
course had no objection; but one
thing or other always prevented her
doing so, and the upshot of the

business was that the priest never saw
him.

Things went on in the old way for
some time longer. The brat continued
yelping and yowling, and eating more
than his three brothers put together,
and playing all sorts of unlucky tricks,
for he was mighty mischievously inclined, till it happened one day that
Tim Carrol, the blind piper, going his
rounds, called in and sat down by the
fire to have a bit of chat with the
woman of the house. So after some
time Tim, who was no churl of his
music, yoked on the pipes, and began
to bellows away in high style; when
the instant he began, the young fellow,
who had been lying as still as a mouse
in his cradle, sat up, began to grin and
twist his ugly face, to swing about his
long tawny arms, and to kick out his
crooked legs, and to show signs of
great glee at the music. At last
nothing would serve him but he should
get the pipes into his own hands, and

to humour him his mother asked Tim to lend them to the child for a minute. Tim, who was kind to children, readily consented; and as Tim had not his sight, Judy herself brought them to the cradle, and went to put them on him; but she had no occasion, for the youth seemed quite up to the business. He buckled on the pipes, set the bellows under one arm, and the bag under the other, worked them both as knowingly as if he had been twenty years at the business, and lilted up 'Sheela na guira' in the finest style imaginable.

All were in astonishment: the poor woman crossed herself. Tim, who, as I said before, was *dark*, and did not well know who was playing, was in great delight; and when he heard that it was a little *prechan* not five years old, that had never seen a set of pipes in his life, he wished the mother joy of her son; offered to take him off her hands if she would part with him, swore he was a *born* piper, a natural *genus*, and declared that in a little time more, with the help of a little good instruction from himself, there would not be his match in the whole country. The poor woman was greatly delighted to hear all this, particularly as what Tim said about natural *genus* quieted some misgivings that were rising in her mind, lest what the neighbours said about his not being right might be too true; and it gratified her moreover to think that her dear child (for she really loved the whelp) would not be forced to turn out and beg, but might earn decent bread for himself. So when Mick came home in the evening from his work, she up and told him all that had happened, and all that Tim Carrol had said; and Mick, as was natural, was very glad to hear it, for the helpless condition of the poor creature was a great trouble to him.   So next day he took the pig to the fair, and with what it brought

set off to Clonmel, and bespoke a
bran-new set of pipes, of the proper
size for him.

In about a fortnight the pipes came
home, and the moment the chap in
his cradle laid eyes on them he squealed
with delight and threw up his pretty
legs, and bumped himself in his cradle,
and went on with a great many comical
tricks; till at last, to quiet him, they
gave him the pipes, and he immediately
set to and pulled away at 'Jig Polthog,'
to the admiration of all who heard him.

The fame of his skill on the pipes
soon spread far and near, for there
was not a piper in the six next counties
could come at all near him, in 'Old
Moderagh rue,' or 'The Hare in the
Corn,' or 'The Fox-hunter's Jig,' or
'The Rakes of Cashel,' or 'The Piper's
Maggot,' or any of the fine Irish jigs
which make people dance whether
they will or no: and it was surprising
to hear him rattle away 'The Fox-
hunt'; you'd really think you heard

the hounds giving tongue, and the terriers yelping always behind, and the huntsman and the whippers-in cheering or correcting the dogs; it was, in short, the very next thing to seeing the hunt itself.

The best of him was, he was noways stingy of his music, and many a merry dance the boys and girls of the neighbourhood used to have in his father's cabin; and he would play up music for them, that they said used as it were to put quicksilver in their feet; and they all declared they never moved so light and so airy to any piper's playing that ever they danced to.

But besides all his fine Irish music, he had one queer tune of his own, the oddest that ever was heard; for the moment he began to play it everything in the house seemed disposed to dance; the plates and porringers used to jingle on the dresser, the pots and pot-hooks used to rattle in the chimney,

and people used even to fancy they
felt the stools moving from under
them ; but, however it might be with
the stools, it is certain that no one
could keep long sitting on them, for
both old and young always fell to
capering as hard as ever they could.
The girls complained that when he
began this tune it always threw them
out in their dancing, and that they
never could handle their feet rightly,
for they felt the floor like ice under
them, and themselves every moment
ready to come sprawling on their
backs or their faces. The young
bachelors who wished to show off their
dancing and their new pumps, and
their bright red or green and yellow
garters, swore that it confused them so
that they never could go rightly through
the *heel and toe* or *cover the buckle*, or
any of their best steps, but felt themselves always all bedizzied and be-
wildered, and then old and young
would go jostling and knocking to-

gether in a frightful manner; and when the unlucky brat had them all in this way, whirligigging about the floor, he'd grin and chuckle and chatter, for all the world like Jacko the monkey when he has played off some of his roguery.

The older he grew the worse he grew, and by the time he was six years old there was no standing the house for him; he was always making his brothers burn or scald themselves, or break their shins over the pots and stools. One time, in harvest, he was left at home by himself, and when his mother came in she found the cat a-horseback on the dog, with her face to the tail, and her legs tied round him, and the urchin playing his queer tune to them; so that the dog went barking and jumping about, and puss was mewing for the dear life, and slapping her tail backwards and forwards, which, as it would hit against the dog's chaps, he'd snap at and bite, and then there was the philliloo. Another time, the farmer with whom Mick worked, a very decent, respectable man, happened to call in, and Judy wiped a stool with her apron, and invited him to sit down and rest himself after· his walk. He was sitting with his back to the cradle, and behind him was a pan of blood, for Judy was making pig's puddings. The lad lay quite still in his nest, and watched his opportunity till he got ready a hook at the end of a piece of twine, which he contrived to fling so handily that it caught in the bob of the man's nice new wig, and soused it in the pan of blood. Another time his mother was coming in from milking the cow, with the pail on her head : the minute he saw her he lilted up his infernal tune, and the poor woman, letting go the pail, clapped her hands aside, and began to dance a jig, and tumbled the milk all a-top of her husband, who was bringing in some turf to boil the supper. In

short, there would be no end to telling
all his pranks, and all the mischievous
tricks he played.

Soon after, some mischances began
to happen to the farmer's cattle. A
horse took the staggers, a fine veal calf
died of the black-leg, and some of his
sheep of the red-water ; the cows began
to grow vicious, and to kick down the
milk-pails, and the roof of one end of
the barn fell in ; and the farmer took
it into his head that Mick Flannigan's
unlucky child was the cause of all the
mischief. So one day he called Mick
aside, and said to him, ' Mick, you see
things are not going on with me as
they ought, and to be plain with you,
Mick, I think that child of yours is the
cause of it. I am really falling away
to nothing with fretting, and I can
hardly sleep on my bed at night for
thinking of what may happen before
the morning. So I'd be glad if you'd
look out for work somewhere else ;
you're as good a man as any in the

country, and there's no fear but you'll have your choice of work.' To this Mick replied, 'that he was sorry for his losses, and still sorrier that he or his should be thought to be the cause of them; that for his own part he was not quite easy in his mind about that child, but he had him and so must keep him'; and he promised to look out for another place immediately.

Accordingly, next Sunday at chapel Mick gave out that he was about leaving the work at John Riordan's, and immediately a farmer who lived a couple of miles off, and who wanted a ploughman (the last one having just left him), came up to Mick, and offered him a house and garden, and work all the year round. Mick, who knew him to be a good employer, immediately closed with him; so it was agreed that the farmer should send a car[1] to take his little bit of furniture, and that

[1] Car, a cart.

he should remove on the following Thursday.

When Thursday came, the car came according to promise, and Mick loaded it, and put the cradle with the child and his pipes on the top, and Judy sat beside it to take care of him, lest he should tumble out and be killed. They drove the cow before them, the dog followed, but the cat was of course left behind; and the other three children went along the road picking skeehories (haws) and blackberries, for it was a fine day towards the latter end of harvest.

They had to cross a river, but as it ran through a bottom between two high banks, you did not see it till you were close on it. The young fellow was lying pretty quiet in the bottom of the cradle, till they came to the head of the bridge, when hearing the roaring of the water (for there was a great flood in the river, as it had rained heavily for the last two or three days),

he sat up in his cradle and looked
about him; and the instant he got a
sight of the water, and found they
were going to take him across it, oh,
how he did bellow and how he did
squeal! no rat caught in a snap-trap
ever sang out equal to him. 'Whist!
A lanna,' said Judy, 'there's no fear
of you; sure it's only over the stone
bridge we're going.'—'Bad luck to
you, you old rip!' cried he, 'what a
pretty trick you've played me to bring
me here!' and still went on yelling,
and the farther they got on the bridge
the louder he yelled; till at last Mick
could hold out no longer, so giving
him a great skelp of the whip he had
in his hand, 'Devil choke you, you
brat!' said he, 'will you never stop
bawling? a body can't hear their ears
for you.' The moment he felt the
thong of the whip he leaped up in the
cradle, clapped the pipes under his
arm, gave a most wicked grin at Mick,
and jumped clean over the battlements

of the bridge down into the water. 'Oh, my child, my child!' shouted Judy, 'he's gone for ever from me.' Mick and the rest of the children ran to the other side of the bridge, and looking over, they saw him coming out from under the arch of the bridge, sitting cross-legged on the top of a white-headed wave, and playing away on the pipes as merrily as if nothing had happened. The river was running very rapidly, so he was whirled away at a great rate; but he played as fast, ay, and faster, than the river ran; and though they set off as hard as they could along the bank, yet, as the river made a sudden turn round the hill, about a hundred yards below the bridge, by the time they got there he was out of sight, and no one ever laid eyes on him more; but the general opinion was that he went home with the pipes to his own relations, the good people, to make music for them.

A FAIRY ENCHANTMENT

Story-teller—MICHAEL HART
Recorder—W. B. YEATS

IN the times when we used to travel by canal I was coming down from Dublin. When we came to Mullingar the canal ended, and I began to walk, and stiff and fatigued I was after the slowness. I had some friends with me, and now and then we walked, now and then we rode in a cart. So on till we saw some girls milking a cow, and stopped to joke with them. After a while we asked them for a drink of milk. 'We have nothing to

E

put it in here,' they said, 'but come to
the house with us.' We went home
with them and sat round the fire talking.
After a while the others went, and left
me, loath to stir from the good fire. I
asked the girls for something to eat.
There was a pot on the fire, and they
took the meat out and put it on a
plate and told me to eat only the meat
that came from the head. When I
had eaten, the girls went out and I
did not see them again.

It grew darker and darker, and there
I still sat, loath as ever to leave the
good fire; and after a while two men
came in, carrying between them a
corpse. When I saw them I hid
behind the door. Says one to the
other, 'Who'll turn the spit?' Says
the other, 'Michael Hart, come out of
that and turn the meat!' I came out
in a tremble and began turning the
spit. 'Michael Hart,' says the one
who spoke first, 'if you let it burn
we will have to put you on the spit

instead,' and on that they went out.
I sat there trembling and turning the
corpse until midnight.   The men came
again, and the one said it was burnt,
and the other said it was done right,
but having fallen out over it, they both
said they would do me no harm that
time; and sitting by the fire one of
them cried out, ' Michael Hart, can you
tell a story?'   'Never a one,' said I.
On that he caught me by the shoulders
and put me out like a shot.

It was a wild, blowing night; never
in all my born days did I see such
a night—the darkest night that ever
came out of the heavens.   I did not
know where I was for the life of me.
So when one of the men came after
me and touched me on the shoulder
with a ' Michael Hart, can you tell a
story now?'—'I can,' says I.   In he
brought me, and, putting me by the
fire, says ' Begin.'   'I have no story
but the one,' says I, 'that I was sitting
here, and that you two men brought

in a corpse and put it on the spit and set me turning it.' 'That will do,' says he; 'you may go in there and lie down on the bed.' And in I went, nothing loath, and in the morning where was I but in the middle of a green field.

TEIGUE OF THE LEE

By Crofton Croker

'I CAN'T stop in the house —I won't stop in it for all the money that is buried in the old castle of Carrigrohan. If ever there was such a thing in the world !—to be abused to my face night and day, and nobody to the fore doing it ! and then, if I'm angry, to be laughed at with a great roaring ho, ho, ho ! I won't stay in the house after to-night, if there was not another place in the country to put my head under.' This angry soliloquy was pronounced in the hall

of the old manor-house of Carrigrohan
by John Sheehan.   John was a new
servant ; he had been only three days
in the house, which had the character
of being haunted, and in that short
space of time he had been abused and
laughed at by a voice which sounded
as if a man spoke with his head in a
cask ; nor could he discover who was
the speaker, or from whence the voice
came.   ' I'll not stop here,' said John ;
' and that ends the matter.'

'Ho, ho, ho! be quiet, John
Sheehan, or else worse will happen to
you.'

John instantly ran to the hall
window, as the words were evidently
spoken by a person immediately outside, but no one was visible.   He had
scarcely placed his face at the pane of
glass when he heard another loud ' Ho,
ho, ho!' as if behind him in the hall ;
as quick as lightning he turned his
head, but no living thing was to be
seen.

'Ho, ho, ho, John!' shouted a voice that appeared to come from the lawn before the house: 'do you think you'll see Teigue?—oh, never! as long as you live! so leave alone looking after him, and mind your business; there's plenty of company to dinner from Cork to be here to-day, and 'tis time you had the cloth laid.'

'Lord bless us! there's more of it! —I'll never stay another day here,' repeated John.

'Hold your tongue, and stay where you are quietly, and play no tricks on Mr. Pratt, as you did on Mr. Jervois about the spoons.'

John Sheehan was confounded by this address from his invisible persecutor, but nevertheless he mustered courage enough to say, 'Who are you? come here, and let me see you, if you are a man'; but he received in reply only a laugh of unearthly derision, which was followed by a 'Good-bye—I'll watch you at dinner, John!'

'Lord between us and harm! this beats all! I'll watch you at dinner! maybe you will! 'tis the broad day-light, so 'tis no ghost; but this is a terrible place, and this is the last day I'll stay in it. How does he know about the spoons? if he tells it I'm a ruined man! there was no living soul could tell it to him but Tim Barrett, and he's far enough off in the wilds of Botany Bay now, so how could he know it? I can't tell for the world! But what's that I see there at the corner of the wall! 'tis not a man! oh, what a fool I am! 'tis only the old stump of a tree! But this is a shock-ing place—I'll never stop in it, for I'll leave the house to-morrow; the very look of it is enough to frighten any one.'

The mansion had certainly an air of desolation; it was situated in a lawn, which had nothing to break its uniform level save a few tufts of narcissuses and a couple of old trees coeval with

the building.   The house stood at a
short distance from the road, it was
upwards of a century old, and Time
was doing his work upon it ; its walls
were weather-stained in all colours, its
roof showed various white patches, it
had no look of comfort ; all was dim
and dingy without, and within there
was an air of gloom, of departed and
departing greatness, which harmonised
well with the exterior.   It required all
the exuberance of youth and of gaiety
to remove the impression, almost
amounting to awe, with which you
trod the huge square hall, paced along
the gallery which surrounded the hall,
or explored the long rambling passages
below stairs.   The ballroom, as the
large drawing-room was called, and
several other apartments, were in a
state of decay ; the walls were stained
with damp, and I remember well the
sensation of awe which I felt creeping
over me when, boy as I was, and full
of boyish life and wild and ardent

spirits, I descended to the vaults; all without and within me became chilled beneath their dampness and gloom——their extent, too, terrified me; nor could the merriment of my two schoolfellows, whose father, a respectable clergyman, rented the dwelling for a time, dispel the feelings of a romantic imagination until I once again ascended to the upper regions.

John had pretty well recovered himself as the dinner-hour approached, and several guests arrived. They were all seated at the table, and had begun to enjoy the excellent repast, when a voice was heard in the lawn.

'Ho, ho, ho! Mr. Pratt, won't you give poor Teigue some dinner? ho, ho! a fine company you have there, and plenty of everything that's good; sure you won't forget poor Teigue?'

John dropped the glass he had in his hand.

'Who is that?' said Mr. Pratt's brother, an officer of the artillery.

'That is Teigue,' said Mr. Pratt, laughing, 'whom you must often have heard me mention.'

'And pray, Mr. Pratt,' inquired another gentleman, 'who *is* Teigue?'

'That,' he replied, 'is more than I can tell. No one has ever been able to catch even a glimpse of him. I have been on the watch for a whole evening with three of my sons, yet, although his voice sometimes sounded almost in my ear, I could not see him. I fancied, indeed, that I saw a man in a white frieze jacket pass into the door from the garden to the lawn, but it could be only fancy, for I found the door locked, while the fellow, whoever he is, was laughing at our trouble. He visits us occasionally, and sometimes a long interval passes between his visits, as in the present case; it is now nearly two years since we heard that hollow voice outside the window. He has never done any injury that we know of, and once when he broke a plate, he brought one back exactly like it.'

'It is very extraordinary,' exclaimed several of the company.

'But,' remarked a gentleman to young Mr. Pratt, 'your father said he broke a plate; how did he get it without your seeing him?'

'When he asks for some dinner we put it outside the window and go away; whilst we watch he will not take it, but no sooner have we withdrawn than it is gone.'

'How does he know that you are watching?'

'That's more than I can tell, but he either knows or suspects. One day my brothers Robert and James with myself were in our back parlour, which has a window into the garden, when he came outside and said, "Ho, ho, ho! Master James and Robert and Henry, give poor Teigue a glass of whisky." James went out of the room, filled a glass with whisky, vinegar, and salt, and brought it to him. "Here, Teigue," said he, "come for it now."— "Well, put it down, then, on the step outside the window." This was done, and we stood looking at it. "There, now, go away," he shouted. We retired, but still watched it. "Ho, ho! you are watching Teigue! go out of the room, now, or I won't take it." We went outside the door and returned, the glass was gone, and a moment after we heard him roaring and cursing frightfully. He took away the glass, but the next day it was on the stone step under the window, and there were crumbs of bread in the inside, as if he had put it in his pocket; from that time he has not been heard till to-day.'

'Oh,' said the colonel, 'I'll get a sight of him; you are not used to these things; an old soldier has the best chance, and as I shall finish my dinner with this wing, I'll be ready for him when he speaks next—Mr. Bell, will you take a glass of wine with me?'

'Ho, ho! Mr. Bell,' shouted Teigue. 'Ho, ho! Mr. Bell, you were a Quaker long ago.   Ho, ho! Mr. Bell, you're a pretty boy! a pretty Quaker you were; and now you're no Quaker, nor anything else: ho, ho! Mr. Bell.   And there's Mr. Parkes: to be sure, Mr. Parkes looks mighty fine to-day, with his powdered head, and his grand silk stockings and his bran new rakish-red waistcoat. And there's Mr. Cole: did you ever see such a fellow?   A pretty company you've brought together, Mr. Pratt: kiln-dried Quakers, butter-buying buckeens from Mallow Lane, and a drinking exciseman from the Coal Quay, to meet the great thundering artillery general that is come out of the Indies, and is the biggest dust of them all.'

'You   scoundrel!'   exclaimed   the colonel, 'I'll make you show your-self'; and snatching up his sword from a corner of the room, he sprang out of the window upon the lawn.   In a moment a shout of laughter, so hollow, so unlike any human sound, made him stop, as well as Mr. Bell, who with a huge oak stick was close at the colonel's heels ; others of the party followed to the lawn, and the remainder rose and went to the windows. 'Come on, colonel,' said Mr. Bell ; 'let us catch this impudent rascal.'

'Ho, ho! Mr. Bell, here I am— here's Teigue—why don't you catch him? Ho, ho! Colonel Pratt, what a pretty soldier you are to draw your sword upon poor Teigue, that never did anybody harm.'

'Let us see your face, you scoundrel,' said the colonel.

'Ho, ho, ho!—look at me—look at me: do you see the wind, Colonel Pratt? you'll see Teigue as soon ; so go in and finish your dinner.'

'If you're upon the earth, I'll find you, you villain!' said the colonel, whilst the same unearthly shout of derision seemed to come from be- hind an angle of the building. 'He's

round that corner,' said Mr. Bell,
'run, run.'

They followed the sound, which was
continued at intervals along the garden
wall, but could discover no human
being; at last both stopped to draw
breath, and in an instant, almost at
their ears, sounded the shout—

'Ho, ho, ho! Colonel Pratt, do you
see Teigue now? do you hear him?
Ho, ho, ho! you're a fine colonel to
follow the wind.'

'Not that way, Mr. Bell—not that
way; come here,' said the colonel.

'Ho, ho, ho! what a fool you are;
do you think Teigue is going to show
himself to you in the field, there?
But, colonel, follow me if you can:
you a soldier! ho, ho, ho!' The
colonel was enraged: he followed the
voice over hedge and ditch, alternately
laughed at and taunted by the unseen
object of his pursuit (Mr. Bell, who
was heavy, was soon thrown out);
until at length, after being led a weary

chase, he found himself at the top of the cliff, over that part of the river Lee, which, from its great depth, and the blackness of its water, has received the name of Hell-hole. Here, on the edge of the cliff, stood the colonel out of breath, and mopping his forehead with his handkerchief, while the voice, which seemed close at his feet, exclaimed, 'Now, Colonel Pratt, now, if you're a soldier, here's a leap for you! Now look at Teigue—why don't you look at him? Ho, ho, ho! Come along; you're warm, I'm sure, Colonel Pratt, so come in and cool yourself; Teigue is going to have a swim!' The voice seemed as if descending amongst the trailing ivy and brushwood which clothes this picturesque cliff nearly from top to bottom, yet it was impossible that any human being could have found footing. 'Now, colonel, have you courage to take the leap? Ho, ho, ho! what a pretty soldier you are. Good-bye; I'll see you again in ten

F

minutes above, at the house—look at your watch, colonel : there's a dive for you'; and a heavy plunge into the water was heard. The colonel stood still, but no sound followed, and he walked slowly back to the house, not quite half a mile from the Crag.

'Well, did you see Teigue?' said his brother, whilst his nephews, scarcely able to smother their laughter, stood by.

'Give me some wine,' said the colonel. 'I never was led such a dance in my life; the fellow carried me all round and round till he brought me to the edge of the cliff, and then down he went into Hell-hole, telling me he'd be here in ten minutes; 'tis more than that now, but he's not come.'

'Ho, ho, ho! colonel, isn't he here? Teigue never told a lie in his life : but, Mr. Pratt, give me a drink and my dinner, and then good-night to you all, for I'm tired; and that's the colonel's doing.' A plate of food was ordered; it was placed by John, with fear and trembling, on the lawn under the window. Every one kept on the watch, and the plate remained undisturbed for some time.

'Ah! Mr. Pratt, will you starve poor Teigue? Make every one go away from the windows, and Master Henry out of the tree, and Master Richard off the garden wall.'

The eyes of the company were turned to the tree and the garden wall; the two boys' attention was occupied in getting down; the visitors were looking at them; and ' Ho, ho, ho!— good luck to you, Mr. Pratt! 'tis a good dinner, and there's the plate, ladies and gentlemen. Good-bye to you, colonel!—good-bye, Mr. Bell! good-bye to you all!' brought their attention back, when they saw the empty plate lying on the grass; and Teigue's voice was heard no more for that evening.   Many visits were afterwards paid by Teigue ; but never was he seen, nor was any discovery ever made of his person or character.

THE FAIRY GREYHOUND

ADDY M'DERMID was one of the most rollicking boys in the whole county of Kildare. Fair or pattern [1] wouldn't be held barring he was in the midst of it. He was in every place, like bad luck, and his poor little farm was seldom sowed in season; and where he expected barley, there grew nothing but weeds. Money became scarce in poor Paddy's pocket; and the cow went after the pig, until nearly

[1] A merry-making in the honour of some patron saint.

all he had was gone. Lucky however
for him, if he had *gomch* (sense) enough
to mind it, he had a most beautiful
dream one night as he lay tossicated
(drunk) in the Rath [1] of Monogue, because he wasn't able to come home.
He dreamt that, under the place where
he lay, a pot of money was buried
since long before the memory of man.
Paddy kept the dream to himself until
the next night, when, taking a spade
and pickaxe, with a bottle of holy water,
he went to the Rath, and, having made
a circle round the place, commenced
diggin' sure enough, for the bare life
and sowl of him thinkin' that he was
made up for ever and ever. He had
sunk about twice the depth of his
knees, when *whack* the pickaxe struck
against a flag, and at the same time
Paddy heard something breathe quite
near him. He looked up, and just

[1] Raths are little fields enclosed by circular
ditches. They are thought to be the sheepfolds and dwellings of an ancient people.

"FORNENT HIM THERE SAT ON HIS HAUNCHES A
COMELY-LOOKING GREYHOUND."   [*Page* 71.

fornent him there sat on his haunches a comely-looking greyhound.

'God save you,' said Paddy, every hair in his head standing up as straight as a sally twig.

'Save you kindly,' answered the greyhound — leaving out God, the beast, bekase he was the divil. Christ defend us from ever seeing the likes o' him.

'Musha, Paddy M'Dermid,' said he, 'what would you be looking after in that grave of a hole you're diggin' there ?'

'Faith, nothing at all, at all,' answered Paddy ; bekase you see he didn't like the stranger.

'Arrah, be easy now, Paddy M'Dermid,' said the greyhound; 'don't I know very well what you are looking for ?'

'Why then in truth, if you do, I may as well tell you at wonst, particularly as you seem a civil-looking gentleman, that's not above speak-

ing to a poor gossoon like myself.'
(Paddy wanted to butter him up a
bit.)

'Well then,' said the greyhound,
'come out here and sit down on this
bank,' and Paddy, like a gomulagh
(fool), did as he was desired, but had
hardly put his brogue outside of the
circle made by the holy water, when
the beast of a hound set upon him,
and drove him out of the Rath; for
for Paddy was frightened, as well he
might, at the fire that flamed from
his mouth. But next night he returned, full sure the money was there.
As before, he made a circle, and
touched the flag, when my gentleman,
the greyhound, appeared in the ould
place.

'Oh ho,' said Paddy, 'you are there,
are you? but it will be a long day,
I promise you, before you trick me
again'; and he made another stroke
at the flag.

'Well, Paddy M'Dermid,' said the

hound, 'since you will have money, you must; but say, how much will satisfy you?'

Paddy scratched his conlaan, and after a while said—

'How much will your honour give me?' for he thought it better to be civil.

'Just as much as you consider reasonable, Paddy M'Dermid.'

'Egad,' says Paddy to himself, 'there's nothing like axin' enough.'

'Say fifty thousand pounds,' said he. (He might as well have said a hundred thousand, for I'll be bail the beast had money gulloure.)

'You shall have it,' said the hound; and then, after trotting away a little bit, he came back with a crock full of guineas between his paws.

'Come here and reckon them,' said he; but Paddy was up to him, and refused to stir, so the crock was shoved alongside the blessed and holy circle, and Paddy pulled it in, right glad to have it in his clutches, and never stood still until he reached his own home, where his guineas turned into little bones, and his ould mother laughed at him. Paddy now swore vengeance against the deceitful beast of a greyhound, and went next night to the Rath again, where, as before, he met Mr. Hound.

'So you are here again, Paddy?' said he.

'Yes, you big blaggard,' said Paddy, 'and I'll never leave this place until I pull out the pot of money that's buried here.'

'Oh, you won't,' said he. 'Well, Paddy M'Dermid, since I see you are such a brave venturesome fellow I'll be after making you up if you walk downstairs with me out of the could'; and sure enough it was snowing like murder.

'Oh may I never see Athy if I do,' returned Paddy, 'for you only want to be loading me with ould bones, or perhaps breaking my own, which would be just as bad.'

''Pon honour,' said the hound, 'I am your friend; and so don't stand in your own light; come with me and your fortune is made. Remain where you are and you'll die a beggar-man.' So bedad, with one palaver and another, Paddy consented; and in the middle of the Rath opened up a beautiful staircase, down which they walked; and after winding and turning they came to a house much finer than the Duke of Leinster's, in which all the tables and chairs were solid gold. Paddy was delighted; and after sitting down, a fine lady handed him a glass of something to drink; but he had hardly swallowed a spoonful when all around set up a horrid yell, and those who before appeared beautiful now looked like what they were—enraged 'good people' (fairies). Before Paddy could bless himself, they seized him, legs and arms, carried him out to a great high hill that stood like a wall over a river, and flung him down. 'Murder!' cried Paddy; but it was no use, no use; he fell upon a rock, and lay there as dead until next morning, where some people found him in the trench that surrounds the *mote* of Coul-hall, the 'good people' having carried him there; and from that hour to the day of his death he was the greatest object in the world. He walked double, and had his mouth (God bless us) where his ear should be.

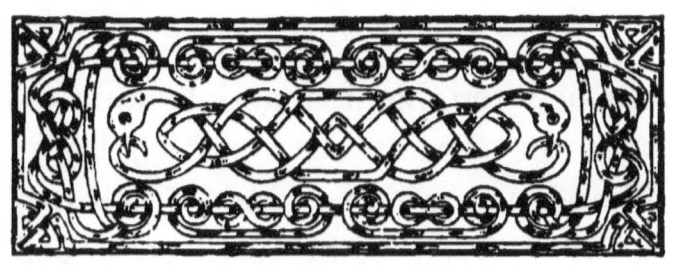

THE LADY OF GOLLERUS

BY CROFTON CROKER

ON the shore of Smerwick harbour, one fine summer's morning, just at daybreak, stood Dick Fitzgerald 'shoghing the dudeen,' which may be translated, smoking his pipe. The sun was gradually rising behind the lofty Brandon, the dark sea was getting green in the light, and the mists clearing away out of the valleys went rolling and curling like the smoke from the corner of Dick's mouth.

''Tis just the pattern of a pretty morning,' said Dick, taking the pipe from between his lips, and looking towards the distant ocean, which lay as still and tranquil as a tomb of polished marble. 'Well, to be sure,' continued he, after a pause, ''tis mighty lonesome to be talking to one's self by way of company, and not to have another soul to answer one—nothing but the child of one's own voice, the echo! I know this, that if I had the luck, or may be the misfortune,' said Dick, with a melancholy smile, 'to have the woman, it would not be this way with me! and what in the wide world is a man without a wife? He's no more surely than a bottle without a drop of drink in it, or dancing without music, or the left leg of a scissors, or a fishing-line without a hook, or any other matter that is no ways complete. Is it not so?' said Dick Fitzgerald, casting his eyes towards a rock upon the strand, which, though it could not speak, stood up as firm and looked as bold as ever Kerry witness did.

But what was his astonishment at beholding, just at the foot of that rock, a beautiful young creature combing her hair, which was of a sea-green colour; and now the salt water shining on it appeared, in the morning light, like melted butter upon cabbage.

Dick guessed at once that she was a Merrow,[1] although he had never seen one before, for he spied the *cohuleen driuth*, or little enchanted cap, which the sea people use for diving down into the ocean, lying upon the strand near her; and he had heard that, if once he could possess himself of the cap she would lose the power of going away into the water: so he seized it with all speed, and she, hearing the noise, turned her head about as natural as any Christian.

When the Merrow saw that her little diving-cap was gone, the salt tears —doubly salt, no doubt, from her— came trickling down her cheeks, and

[1] Sea fairy.

she began a low mournful cry with just the tender voice of a new-born infant. Dick, although he knew well enough what she was crying for, determined to keep the *cohuleen driuth*, let her cry never so much, to see what luck would come out of it. Yet he could not help pitying her ; and when the dumb thing looked up in his face, with her cheeks all moist with tears, 'twas enough to make any one feel, let alone Dick, who had ever and always, like most of his countrymen, a mighty tender heart of his own.

'Don't cry, my darling,' said Dick Fitzgerald ; but the Merrow, like any bold child, only cried the more for that.

Dick sat himself down by her side, and took hold of her hand by way of comforting her. 'Twas in no particular an ugly hand, only there was a small web between the fingers, as there is in a duck's foot ; but 'twas as thin and as white as the skin between egg and shell.

'What's your name, my darling?'
says Dick, thinking to make her con-
versant with him; but he got no
answer; and he was certain sure now,
either that she could not speak, or
did not understand him: he therefore
squeezed her hand in his, as the only
way he had of talking to her. It's the
universal language; and there's not a
woman in the world, be she fish or
lady, that does not understand it.

The Merrow did not seem much
displeased at this mode of conversa-
tion; and making an end of her whin-
ing all at once, 'Man,' says she, looking up in Dick Fitzgerald's face; 'man,
will you eat me?'

'By all the red petticoats and check
aprons between Dingle and Tralee,'
cried Dick, jumping up in amazement,
'I'd as soon eat myself, my jewel!
Is it I eat you, my pet? Now, 'twas
some ugly ill-looking thief of a fish put
that notion into your own pretty head,
with the nice green hair down upon it,

G

that is so cleanly combed out this morning!'

'Man,' said the Merrow, 'what will you do with me if you won't eat me?'

Dick's thoughts were running on a wife: he saw, at the first glimpse, that she was handsome; but since she spoke, and spoke too like any real woman, he was fairly in love with her. 'Twas the neat way she called him man that settled the matter entirely.

'Fish,' says Dick, trying to speak to her after her own short fashion; 'fish,' says he, 'here's my word, fresh and fasting, for you this blessed morning, that I'll make you Mistress Fitzgerald before all the world, and that's what I'll do.'

'Never say the word twice,' says she; 'I'm ready and willing to be yours, Mister Fitzgerald; but stop, if you please, till I twist up my hair.' It was some time before she had settled it entirely to her liking; for she guessed, I suppose, that she was going among

strangers, where she would be looked
at. When that was done, the Merrow
put the comb in her pocket, and then
bent down her head and whispered
some words to the water that was close
to the foot of the rock.

Dick saw the murmur of the words
upon the top of the sea, going out
towards the wide ocean, just like a
breath of wind rippling along, and,
says he, in the greatest wonder, ' Is it
speaking you are, my darling, to the ·
salt water ? '

' It's nothing else,' says she, quite
carelessly ; ' I'm just sending word
home to my father not to be waiting
breakfast for me ; just to keep him
from being uneasy in his mind.'

' And who's your father, my duck ? '
said Dick.

' What ! ' said the Merrow, ' did you
never hear of my father ? he's the king
of the waves to be sure ! '

' And yourself, then, is a real king's
daughter ? ' said Dick, opening his two

eyes to take a full and true survey of
his wife that was to be. 'Oh, I'm
nothing else but a made man with
you, and a king your father; to be
sure he has all the money that's down
at the bottom of the sea!'

'Money,' repeated the Merrow,
'what's money?'

''Tis no bad thing to have when one
wants it,' replied Dick; 'and may be
now the fishes have the understanding
to bring up whatever you bid them?'

'Oh yes,' said the Merrow, 'they
bring me what I want.'

'To speak the truth then,' said Dick,
''tis a straw bed I have at home before
you, and that, I'm thinking, is no ways
fitting for a king's daughter; so if
'twould not be displeasing to you,
just to mention a nice feather bed,
with a pair of new blankets—but
what am I talking about? may be you
have not such things as beds down
under the water?'

'By all means,' said she, 'Mr.

Fitzgerald—plenty of beds at your service. I've fourteen oyster-beds of my own, not to mention one just planting for the rearing of young ones.'

'You have?' says Dick, scratching his head and looking a little puzzled. '"Tis a feather bed I was speaking of; but, clearly, yours is the very cut of a decent plan to have bed and supper so handy to each other, that a person when they'd have the one need never ask for the other.'

However, bed or no bed, money or no money, Dick Fitzgerald determined to marry the Merrow, and the Merrow had given her consent. Away they went, therefore, across the strand, from Gollerus to Ballinrunnig, where Father Fitzgibbon happened to be that morning.

'There are two words to this bargain, Dick Fitzgerald,' said his Reverence, looking mighty glum. 'And is it a fishy woman you'd marry? The Lord preserve us! Send the scaly creature home to her own people; that's my advice to you, wherever she came from.'

Dick had the *cohuleen driuth* in his hand, and was about to give it back to the Merrow, who looked covetously at it, but he thought for a moment, and then says he, 'Please your Reverence, she's a king's daughter.'

'If she was the daughter of fifty kings,' said Father Fitzgibbon, 'I tell you, you can't marry her, she being a fish.'

'Please your Reverence,' said Dick again, in an undertone, 'she is as mild and as beautiful as the moon.'

'If she was as mild and as beautiful as the sun, moon, and stars, all put together, I tell you, Dick Fitzgerald,' said the Priest, stamping his right foot, 'you can't marry her, she being a fish.'

'But she has all the gold that's down in the sea only for the asking, and I'm a made man if I marry her; and,' said Dick, looking up slily, 'I can

make it worth any one's while to do
the job.'

'Oh! that alters the case entirely,'
replied the Priest; 'why there's some
reason now in what you say: why
didn't you tell me this before? marry
her by all means, if she was ten times
a fish. Money, you know, is not to
be refused in these bad times, and I
may as well have the hansel of it as
another, that may be would not take
half the pains in counselling you that
I have done.'

So Father Fitzgibbon married Dick
Fitzgerald to the Merrow, and like
any loving couple, they returned to
Gollerus well pleased with each other.
Everything prospered with Dick—he
was at the sunny side of the world;
the Merrow made the best of wives,
and they lived together in the greatest
contentment.

It was wonderful to see, considering
where she had been brought up, how
she would busy herself about the house,

and how well she nursed the children ;
for, at the end of three years there
were as many young Fitzgeralds—two
boys and a girl.

In short, Dick was a happy man,
and so he might have been to the end
of his days if he had only had the
sense to take care of what he had got ;
many another man, however, beside
Dick, has not had wit enough to do
that.

One day, when Dick was obliged to
go to Tralee, he left the wife minding
the children at home after him, and
thinking she had plenty to do without
disturbing his fishing-tackle.

Dick was no sooner gone than Mrs.
Fitzgerald set about cleaning up the
house, and chancing to pull down a
fishing-net, what should she find behind it in a hole in the wall but her
own *cohuleen driuth.* She took it out
and looked at it, and then she thought
of her father the king, and her mother
the queen, and her brothers and sisters,

and she felt a longing to go back to them.

She sat down on a little stool and thought over the happy days she had spent under the sea; then she looked at her children, and thought on the love and affection of poor Dick, and how it would break his heart to lose her. 'But,' says she, 'he won't lose me entirely, for I'll come back to him again, and who can blame me for going to see my father and my mother after being so long away from them?'

She got up and went towards the door, but came back again to look once more at the child that was sleeping in the cradle. She kissed it gently, and as she kissed it a tear trembled for an instant in her eye and then fell on its rosy cheek. She wiped away the tear, and turning to the eldest little girl, told her to take good care of her brothers, and to be a good child herself until she came back. The Merrow then went down to the strand. The

sea was lying calm and smooth, just
heaving and glittering in the sun, and
she thought she heard a faint sweet
singing, inviting her to come down.
All her old ideas and feelings came
flooding over her mind, Dick and her
children were at the instant forgotten,
and placing the *cohuleen driuth* on her
head she plunged in.

Dick came home in the evening, and
missing his wife he asked Kathleen, his
little girl, what had become of her
mother, but she could not tell him.
He then inquired of the neighbours,
and he learned that she was seen going
towards the strand with a strange-
looking thing like a cocked hat in her
hand. He returned to his cabin to
search for the *cohuleen driuth*. It was
gone, and the truth now flashed upon
him.

Year after year did Dick Fitzgerald
wait expecting the return of his wife,
but he never saw her more. Dick
never married again, always thinking

that the Merrow would sooner or later return to him, and nothing could ever persuade him but that her father the king kept her below by main force; 'for,' said Dick, 'she surely would not of herself give up her husband and her children.'

While she was with him she was so good a wife in every respect that to this day she is spoken of in the tradition of the country as the pattern for one, under the name of THE LADY OF GOLLERUS.

EVIL SPIRITS

THE DEVIL'S MILL

By Samuel Lover

YOU see, sir, there was a colonel wanst, in times back, that owned a power of land about here—but God keep uz, they said he didn't come by it honestly, but did a crooked turn whenever 'twas to sarve himself.

Well, the story goes that at last the divil (God bless us) kem to him, and promised him hapes o' money, and all his heart could desire and more, too, if he'd sell his sowl in exchange.

He was too cunnin' for that; bad as he was—and he was bad enough

God knows—he had some regard for his poor sinful sowl, and he would not give himself up to the divil, all out; but, the villain, he thought he might make a bargain with the *old chap*, and get all he wanted, and keep himself out of harm's way still: for he was mighty 'cute—and, throth, he was able for Owld Nick any day.

Well, the bargain was struck, and it was this-a-way: the divil was to give him all the goold ever he'd ask for, and was to let him alone as long as he could; and the timpter promised him a long day, and said 'twould be a great while before he'd want him at all, at all; and whin that time kem, he was to keep his hands aff him, as long as the other could give him some work he couldn't do.

So, when the bargain was made, 'Now,' says the colonel to the divil, 'give me all the money I want.'

'As much as you like,' says Owld Nick; 'how much will you have?'

'You must fill me that room,' says he, pointin' into a murtherin' big room that he emptied out on purpose— 'you must fill that room,' says he, 'up to the very ceilin' with goolden guineas.'

· 'And welkem,' says the divil.

With that, sir, he began to shovel the guineas into the room like mad; and the colonel towld him, that as soon as he was done, to come to him in his own parlour below, and that he would then go up and see if the divil was as good as his word, and had filled the room with the goolden guineas. So the colonel went downstairs, and the owld fellow worked away as busy as a nailer, shovellin' in the guineas by hundherds and thousands.

Well, he worked away for an hour and more, and at last he began to get tired; and he thought it *mighty odd* that the room wasn't fillin' fasther. Well, afther restin' for awhile, he began agin, and he put his shouldher to the work in airnest; but still the room was no fuller at all, at all.

'Och! bad luck to me,' says the divil, 'but the likes of this I never seen,' says he, 'far and near, up and down—the dickens a room I ever kem across afore,' says he, 'I couldn't cram while a cook would be crammin' a turkey, till now; and here I am,' says he, 'losin' my whole day, and I with such a power o' work an my hands yit, and this room no fuller than five minutes ago.'

Begor, while he was spakin' he seen the hape o' guineas in the middle of the flure growing *littler and littler* every minit; and at last they wor disappearing, for all the world like corn in the hopper of a mill.

'Ho! ho!' says Owld Nick, 'is that the way wid you?' says he; and wid that, he ran over to the hape of goold —and what would you think, but it was runnin' down through a great big hole in the flure, that the colonel made

through the ceilin' in the room below ;
and that was the work he was at afther
he left the divil, though he purtended
he was only waitin' for him in his
parlour ; and there the divil, when he
looked down the hole in the flure, seen
the colonel, not content with the *two*
rooms full of guineas, but with a big
shovel throwin' them into a closet a'
one side of him as fast as they fell
down.   So, putting his head through the
hole, he called down to the colonel :

' Hillo, neighbour ! ' says he.

The colonel looked up, and grew as
white as a sheet, when he seen he was
found out, and the red eyes starin'
down at him through the hole.

' Musha, bad luck to your impu-
dence !' says Owld Nick : 'it is sthrivin'
to chate *me* you are,' says he, ' you
villain ! '

' Oh, forgive me for this wanst ! '
says the colonel, ' and, upon the honour
of a gintleman,' says he, ' I'll never
_____ '

'Whisht! whisht! you thievin' rogue,' says the divil, 'I'm not angry with you at all, at all, but only like you the betther, bekase you're so cute;—lave off slaving yourself there,' says he, 'you have got goold enough for this time; and whenever you want more, you have only to say the word, and it shall be yours to command.'

So with that, the divil and he parted for that time: and myself doesn't know whether they used to meet often afther or not; but the colonel never wanted money, anyhow, but went on prosperous in the world—and, as the saying is, if he took the dirt out o' the road, it id turn to money wid him; and so, in course of time, he bought great estates, and was a great man entirely—not a greater in Ireland, throth.

At last, afther many years of prosperity, the owld colonel got stricken in years, and he began to have misgivings in his conscience for his wicked doings, and his heart was heavy as the fear of death came upon him; and sure enough, while he had such murnful thoughts, the divil kem to him, and towld him *he should go wid him.*

Well, to be sure, the owld man was frekened, but he plucked up his courage and his cuteness, and towld the divil, in a bantherin' way, jokin' like, that he had partic'lar business thin, that he was goin' to a party, and hoped an *owld friend* wouldn't inconvaynience him that-a-way.

The divil said he'd call the next day, and that he must be ready; and sure enough in the evenin' he kem to him; and when the colonel seen him, he reminded him of his bargain that as long as he could give him some work he couldn't do, he wasn't obleeged to go.

'That's thrue,' says the divil.

'I'm glad you're as good as your word, anyhow,' says the colonel.

'I never bruk my word yit,' says the owld chap, cocking up his horns consaitedly ; 'honour bright,' says he.

'Well then,' says the colonel, 'build me a mill, down there, by the river,' says he, 'and let me have it finished by to-morrow mornin'.'

'Your will is my pleasure,' says the owld chap, and away he wint ; and the colonel thought he had nicked Owld Nick at last, and wint to bed quite aisy in his mind.

But, *jewel machree*, sure the first thing he heerd the next mornin' was that the whole counthry round was runnin' to see a fine bran new mill that was an the river-side, where the evening before not a thing at all, at all, but rushes was standin', and all, of coorse, wonderin' what brought it there ; and some sayin' 'twas not lucky, and many more throubled in their mind, but one and all agreein' it was no *good*; and that's the very mill forninst you.

But when the colonel heered it he was more throubled than any, of coorse, and began to conthrive what else he could think iv to keep himself out iv the claws of the *owld one*. Well, he often heerd tell that there was one thing the divil never could do, and I darsay you heerd it too, sir, —that is, that he couldn't make a rope out of the sands of the say; and so when the *owld one* kem to him the next day and said his job was done, and that now the mill was built he must either tell him somethin' else he wanted done, or come away wid him.

So the colonel said he saw it was all over wid him. 'But,' says he, 'I wouldn't like to go wid you alive, and sure it's all the same to you, alive or dead?'

'Oh, that won't do,' says his frind; 'I can't wait no more,' says he.

'I don't want you to wait, my dear frind,' says the colonel; 'all I want is, that you'll be plased to kill me before you take me away.'

'With pleasure,' says Owld Nick.

'But will you promise me my choice of dyin' one partic'lar way?' says the colonel.

'Half a dozen ways, if it plazes you,' says he.

'You're mighty obleegin',' says the colonel; 'and so,' says he, 'I'd rather die by bein' hanged with a rope *made out of the sands of the say*,' says he, lookin' mighty knowin' at the *owld fellow*.

'I've always one about me,' says the divil, 'to obleege my frinds,' says he; and with that he pulls out a rope made of sand, sure enough.

'Oh, it's game you're makin',' says the colonel, growin' as white as a sheet.

'The *game is mine*, sure enough,' says the owld fellow, grinnin', with a terrible laugh.

'That's not a sand-rope at all,' says the colonel.

'Isn't it?' says the divil, hittin' him
acrass the face with the ind iv the
rope, and the sand (for it *was* made of
sand, sure enough) went into one of
his eyes, and made the tears come
with the pain.

'That bates all I ever seen or heerd,'
says the colonel, sthrivin' to rally and
make another offer; 'is there anything
you *can't* do?'

'Nothing you can tell me,' says the
divil, 'so you may as well leave off
your palaverin' and come along at
wanst.'

'Will you give me one more offer,'
says the colonel.

'You don't desarve it,' says the
divil; 'but I don't care if I do';
for you see, sir, he was only playin'
wid him, and tantalising the owld
sinner.

'All fair,' says the colonel, and with
that he ax'd him could he stop a
woman's tongue.

'Thry me,' says Owld Nick.

'Well then,' says the colonel, 'make my lady's tongue be quiet for the next month and I'd thank you.'

'She'll never trouble you agin,' says Owld Nick; and with that the colonel heerd roarin' and cryin', and the door of his room was thrown open and in ran his daughter, and fell down at his feet, telling him her mother had just dhropped dead.

The minit the door opened, the divil runs and hides himself behind a big elbow-chair; and the colonel was frekened almost out of his siven sinses by raison of the sudden death of his poor lady, let alone the jeopardy he was in himself, seein' how the divil had *forestalled* him every way; and after ringin' his bell and callin' to his sarvants and recoverin' his daughter out of her faint, he was goin' away wid her out of the room, whin the divil caught howld of him by the skirt of the coat, and the colonel was obleeged to let his daughter be carried

out by the sarvants, and shut the door
afther them.

'Well,' says the divil, and he grinn'd
and wagg'd his tail, all as one as a
dog when he's plaised; 'what do you
say now?' says he.

'Oh,' says the colonel, 'only lave
me alone until I bury my poor wife,'
says he, 'and I'll go with you then,
you villain,' says he.

'Don't call names,' says the divil;
'you had better keep a civil tongue
in your head,' says he; 'and it doesn't
become a gintleman to forget good
manners.'

'Well, sir, to make a long story
short, the divil purtended to let him
off, out of kindness, for three days
antil his wife was buried; but the
raison of it was this, that when the
lady his daughter fainted, he loosened
the clothes about her throat, and in
pulling some of her dhress away, he
tuk off a goold chain that was on
her neck and put it in his pocket,

and the chain had a diamond crass on it (the Lord be praised!) and the divil darn't touch him while he had *the sign of the crass* about him.

Well, the poor colonel (God forgive him!) was grieved for the loss of his lady, and she had an *illigant berrin*— and they say that when the prayers was readin' over the dead, the owld colonel took it to heart like anything, and the word o' God kem home to his poor sinful sowl at last.

Well, sir, to make a long story short, the ind of it was, that for the three days o' grace that was given to him the poor deluded owld sinner did nothin' at all but read the Bible from mornin' till night, and bit or sup didn't pass his lips all the time, he was so intint upon the Holy Book, but he sat up in an owld room in the far ind of the house, and bid no one disturb him an no account, and struv to make his heart bould with the words iv life; and sure it was somethin'

strinthened him at last, though as the
time drew nigh that the *inimy* was to
come, he didn't feel aisy, and no
wondher; and, bedad the three days
was past and gone in no time, and
the story goes that at the dead hour
o' the night, when the poor sinner
was readin' away as fast as he could,
my jew'l, his heart jumped up to his
mouth at gettin' a tap on the shoulder.

'Oh, murther!' says he, 'who's
there?' for he was afeard to look
up.

'It's me,' says the *owld one*, and
he stood right forninst him, and his
eyes like coals o' fire, lookin' him
through, and he said, with a voice
that almost split his owld heart,
'Come!' says he.

'Another day!' cried out the poor
colonel.

'Not another hour,' says Sat'n.

'Half an hour!'

'Not a quarther,' says the divil,
grinnin' with a bitther laugh; 'give

over your readin', I bid you,' says he,
'and come away wid me.'

'Only gi' me a few minits,' says he.

'Lave aff your palaverin', you snakin'
owld sinner,' says Sat'n; 'you know
you're bought and sould to me, and
a purty bargain I have o' you, you
owld baste,' says he; 'so come along
at wanst,' and he put out his claw
to ketch him; but the colonel tuk
a fast hould o' the Bible, and begged
hard that he'd let him alone, and
wouldn't harm him antil the bit o'
candle that was just blinkin' in the
socket before him was burned out.

'Well, have it so, you dirty coward,'
says Owld Nick, and with that he
spit an him.

But the poor owld colonel didn't
lose a minit (for he was cunnin' to
the ind), but snatched the little taste
o' candle that was forninst him out
o' the candlestick, and puttin' it an
the Holy Book before him, he shut
down the cover of it and quinched

the light. With that the divil gave a roar like a bull, and vanished in a flash o' fire, and the poor colonel fainted away in his chair; but the sarvants heerd the noise (for the divil tore aff the roof o' the house when he left it), and run into the room, and brought their master to himself agin. And from that day he was an althered man, and used to have the Bible read to him every day, for he couldn't read himself any more, by raison of losin' his eyesight when the divil hit him with the rope of sand in the face, and afther spit an him—for the sand wint into one eye, and he lost the other that-a-way, savin' your presence.

FERGUS O'MARA AND THE AIR-DEMONS

BY DR. P. W. JOYCE

O F all the different kinds of goblins that haunted the lonely places of Ireland in days of old, air-demons were most dreaded by the people. They lived among clouds, and mists, and rocks, and they hated the human race with the utmost malignity. In those times lived in the north of Desmond (the present county of Cork) a man man named Fergus O'Mara. His farm lay on the southern slope of the Ballyhoura Mountains, along which ran the open road that led to his house. This road was not shut in by walls or fences; but on both sides there were scattered trees and bushes that sheltered it in winter, and made it dark and gloomy when you approached the house at night. Beside the road, a little way off from the house, there was a spot that had an evil name all over the country, a little hill covered closely with copsewood, with a great craggy rock on top, from which, on stormy nights, strange and fearful sounds had often been heard— shrill voices, and screams, mingled with loud fiendish laughter; and the people believed that it was the haunt of air-demons. In some way it had become known that these demons had an eye on Fergus, and watched for every opportunity to get him into their power. He had himself been warned of this many years before, by an old monk from the neighbouring monastery of Buttevant, who told him, moreover,

I

that so long as he led a blameless,
upright life, he need have no fear of
the demons; but that if ever he
yielded to temptation or fell into any
great sin, then would come the
opportunity for which they were
watching day and night. He never
forgot this warning, and he was very
careful to keep himself straight, both
because he was naturally a good man,
and for fear of the air-demons.

Some time before the occurrence
about to be related, one of Fergus's
children, a sweet little girl about seven
years of age, fell ill and died. The
little thing gradually wasted away, but
suffered no pain; and as she grew
weaker she became more loving and
gentle than ever, and talked in a
wonderful way, quite beyond her years,
of the bright land she was going to.
One thing she was particularly anxious
about, that when she was dying they
should let her hold a blessed candle
in her hand. They thought it very

strange that she should be so continu-
ally thinking and talking of this; and
over and over again she made her father
and mother promise that it should be
done. And with the blessed candle
in her hand she died so calmly and
sweetly that those round her bed could
not tell the exact moment.

About a year after this, on a bright
Sunday morning in October, Fergus
set out for Mass. The place was
about three miles away, and it was not
a chapel,[1] but a lonely old fort, called
to this day Lissanaffrin, the fort of the
Mass. A rude stone altar stood at
one side near the mound of the fort,
under a little shed that sheltered the
priest also; and the congregation
worshipped in the open air on the
green plot in the centre. For in those
days there were many places that had
no chapels; and the people flocked to

[1] A fort is the same as a rath (see p. 70);
a few are fenced in with unmortared stone walls
instead of clay ditches.

these open-air Masses as faithfully as
we do now to our stately comfortable
chapels. The family had gone on
before, the men walking and the women
and children riding; and Fergus set
out to walk alone.

Just as he approached the Demons'
Rock he was greatly surprised to hear
the eager yelping of dogs, and in a
moment a great deer bounded from the
covert beside the rock, with three
hounds after her in full chase. No
man in the whole country round loved
a good chase better than Fergus, or
had a swifter foot to follow, and without a moment's hesitation he started
in pursuit. But in a few minutes he
stopped up short; for he bethought
him of the Mass, and he knew there
was little time for delay. While he
stood wavering, the deer seemed to
slacken her pace, and the hounds
gained on her, and in a moment
Fergus dashed off at full speed, forget-
ting Mass and everything else in his

eagerness for the sport. But it turned
out a long and weary chase. Sometimes they slackened, and he was
almost at the hounds' tails, but the
next moment both deer and hounds
started forward and left him far behind.
Sometimes they were in full view, and
again they were out of sight in thickets
and deep glens, so that he could guide
himself only by the cry of the hounds.
In this way he was decoyed across
hills and glens, but instead of gaining
ground he found himself rather falling
behind.

Mass was all over and the people
dispersed to their homes, and all
wondered that they did not see Fergus;
for no one could remember that he
was ever absent before. His wife returned, expecting to find him at home;
but when she arrived there was trouble
in her heart, for there were no tidings
of him, and no one had seen him since
he had set out for Mass in the morning.

Meantime Fergus followed up the

chase till he was wearied out; and at last, just on the edge of a wild moor, both deer and hounds disappeared behind a shoulder of rock, and he lost them altogether. At the same moment the cry of the hounds became changed to frightful shrieks and laughter, such as he had heard more than once from the Demons' Rock. And now, sitting down on a bank to rest, he had full time to reflect on what he had done, and he was overwhelmed with remorse and shame. Moreover, his heart sank within him, thinking of the last sounds he had heard; for he believed that he had been allured from Mass by the cunning wiles of the demons, and he feared that the dangerous time had come foretold by the monk. He started up and set out for his home, hoping to reach it before night. But before he had got half-way night fell and a storm came on, great wind and rain and bursts of thunder and lightning. Fergus was strong and active, however, and knew every turn of the mountain, and he made his way through the storm till he approached the Demons' Rock.

Suddenly there burst on his ears the very same sounds that he had heard on losing sight of the chase—shouts and shrieks and laughter. A great black ragged cloud, whirling round and round with furious gusts of wind, burst from the rock and came sweeping and tearing towards him. Crossing himself in terror and uttering a short prayer, he rushed for home. But the whirlwind swept nearer, till at last, in a sort of dim, shadowy light, he saw the black cloud full of frightful faces, all glaring straight at him and coming closer and closer. At this moment a bright light dropped down from the sky and rested in front of the cloud; and when he looked up, he saw his little child floating in the air between him and the demons, holding a lighted candle in her hand. And although the storm was raging

and roaring all round, she was quite
calm—not a breath of air stirred her
long yellow hair—and the candle
burned quietly.   Even in the midst
of all his terror he could observe her
pale gentle face and blue eyes just as
when she was alive, not showing traces
of sickness or sadness now, but
lighted up with joy.   The demons
seemed to start back from the light,
and with great uproar rushed round to
the other side of Fergus, the black
cloud still moving with them and
wrapping them up in its ragged folds;
but the little angel floated softly
round, still keeping between them and
her father.   Fergus ran on for home,
and the cloud of demons still kept
furiously whirling round and round
him, bringing with them a whirlwind
that roared among the trees and bushes
and tore them from the roots; but
still the child, always holding the
candle towards them, kept floating
calmly round and shielded him.

At length he arrived at his house;
the door lay half-open, for the family
were inside expecting him home, listening with wonder and affright to the
approaching noises; and he bounded
in through the doorway and fell flat on
his face. That instant the door—
though no one was near—was shut
violently, and the bolts were shot home.
They hurried anxiously round him to
lift him up, but found him in a death-
like swoon. Meantime the uproar outside became greater than ever; round
and round the house it tore, a roaring
whirlwind with shouts and yells of rage,
and great trampling, as if there was
a whole company of horsemen. At
length, however, the noises seemed to
move away farther and farther off from
the house, and gradually died away in
the distance. At the same time the
storm ceased, and the night became
calm and beautiful.

The daylight was shining in through
the windows when Fergus recovered

from his swoon, and then he told his fearful story; but many days passed over before he had quite recovered from the horrors of that night. When the family came forth in the morning there was fearful waste all round and near the house, trees and bushes torn from the roots, and the ground all trampled and torn up. After this the revelry of the demons was never again heard from the rock; and it was believed that they had left it and betaken themselves to some other haunt.

THE MAN WHO NEVER KNEW FEAR

Translated from the Gaelic by Douglas Hyde

THERE was once a lady, and she had two sons whose names were Louras (Lawrence) and Carrol. From the day that Lawrence was born nothing ever made him afraid, but Carrol would never go outside the door from the time the darkness of the night began.

It was the custom at that time when a person died for people to watch the dead person's grave in turn, one after another; for there used to be destroyers going about stealing the corpses.

When the mother of Carrol and Lawrence died, Carrol said to Lawrence—

'You say that nothing ever made you afraid yet, but I'll make a bet with you that you haven't courage to watch your mother's tomb to-night.'

'I'll make a bet with you that I have,' said Lawrence.

When the darkness of the night was coming, Lawrence put on his sword and went to the burying-ground. He sat down on a tombstone near his mother's grave till it was far in the night and sleep was coming upon him. Then he saw a big black thing coming to him, and when it came near him he saw that it was a head without a body that was in it. He drew the sword to give it a blow if it should come any nearer, but it didn't come. Lawrence remained looking at it until the light of the day was coming, then the head-without-body went, and Lawrence came home.

Carrol asked him, did he see any-thing in the graveyard.

'I did,' said Lawrence, 'and my mother's body would be gone, but that I was guarding it.'

'Was it dead or alive, the person you saw?' said Carrol.

'I don't know was it dead or alive,' said Lawrence; 'there was nothing in it but a head without a body.'

'Weren't you afraid?' says Carrol.

'Indeed I wasn't,' said Lawrence; 'don't you know that nothing in the world ever put fear on me.'

'I'll bet again with you that you haven't the courage to watch to-night again,' says Carrol.

'I would make that bet with you,' said Lawrence, 'but that there is a night's sleep wanting to me. Go yourself to-night.'

'I wouldn't go to the graveyard

to-night if I were to get the riches of the world,' says Carrol.

'Unless you go your mother's body will be gone in the morning,' says Lawrence.

'If only you watch to-night and to-morrow night, I never will ask of you to do a turn of work as long as you will be alive,' said Carrol, 'but I think there is fear on you.'

'To show you that there's no fear on me,' said Lawrence, 'I will watch.'

He went to sleep, and when the evening came he rose up, put on his sword, and went to the graveyard. He sat on a tombstone near his mother's grave. About the middle of the night he heard a great sound coming. A big black thing came as far as the grave and began rooting up the clay. Lawrence drew back his sword, and with one blow he made two halves of the big black thing, and with the second blow he made two halves of each half, and he saw it no more.

Lawrence went home in the morning, and Carrol asked him did he see anything.

'I did,' said Lawrence, 'and only that I was there my mother's body would be gone.'

'Is it the head-without-body that came again?' said Carrol.

'It was not, but a big black thing, and it was digging up my mother's grave until I made two halves of it.'

Lawrence slept that day, and when the evening came he rose up, put on his sword, and went to the churchyard. He sat down on a tombstone until it was the middle of the night. Then he saw a thing as white as snow and as hateful as sin; it had a man's head on it, and teeth as long as a flax-carder. Lawrence drew back the sword and was going to deal it a blow, when it said—

'Hold your hand; you have saved your mother's body, and there is not a man in Ireland as brave as you.

There is great riches waiting for you if you go looking for it.'

Lawrence went home, and Carrol asked him did he see anything.

'I did,' said Lawrence, 'and but that I was there my mother's body would be gone, but there's no fear of it now.'

In the morning, the day on the morrow, Lawrence said to Carrol—

'Give me my share of money, and I'll go on a journey, until I have a look round the country.'

Carrol gave him the money, and he went walking. He went on until he came to a large town. He went into the house of a baker to get bread. The baker began talking to him, and asked him how far he was going.

'I am going looking for something that will put fear on me,' said Lawrence.

'Have you much money?' said the baker.

'I have a half-hundred pounds,' said Lawrence.

'I'll bet another half-hundred with you that there will be fear on you if you go to the place that I'll bid you,' says the baker.

'I'll take your bet,' said Lawrence, 'if only the place is not too far away from me.'

'It's not a mile from the place where you're standing,' said the baker; 'wait here till the night comes, and then go to the graveyard, and as a sign that you were in it, bring me the goblet that is upon the altar of the old church (*cill*) that is in the grave-yard.'

When the baker made the bet he was certain that he would win, for there was a ghost in the churchyard, and nobody went into it for forty years before that whom he did not kill.

When the darkness of the night came, Lawrence put on his sword and went to the burying-ground. He

K

came to the door of the churchyard
and struck it with his sword. The
door opened, and there came out a
great black ram, and two horns on
him as long as flails. Lawrence gave
him a blow, and he went out of sight,
leaving him up to the two ankles in
blood. Lawrence went into the old
church, got the goblet, came back
to the baker's house, gave him the
goblet, and got the bet. Then the
baker asked him did he see anything
in the churchyard.

'I saw a big black ram with long
horns on him,' said Lawrence, 'and
I gave him a blow which drew as
much blood out of him as would
swim a boat; sure he must be dead
by this time.'

In the morning, the day on the
morrow, the baker and a lot of people
went to the graveyard and they saw
the blood of the black ram at the
door. They went to the priest and
told him that the black ram was

banished out of the churchyard. The
priest did not believe them, because
the churchyard was shut up forty years
before that on account of the ghost
that was in it, and neither priest nor
friar could banish him. The priest came
with them to the door of the churchyard, and when he saw the blood he
took courage and sent for Lawrence,
and heard the story from his own
mouth. Then he sent for his blessing-
materials, and desired the people to
come in till he read mass for them.
The priest went in, and Lawrence and
the people after him, and he read mass
without the big black ram coming as
he used to do. The priest was greatly
rejoiced, and gave Lawrence another
fifty pounds.

On the morning of the next day
Lawrence went on his way. He
travelled the whole day without seeing
a house. About the hour of midnight
he came to a great lonely valley, and
he saw a large gathering of people

looking at two men hurling. Lawrence
stood looking at them, as there was
a bright light from the moon. It
was the good people that were in
it, and it was not long until one of
them struck a blow on the ball and
sent it into Lawrence's breast. He
put his hand in after the ball to draw
it out, and what was there in it but the
head of a man. When Lawrence got
a hold of it, it began screeching, and
at last it asked Lawrence—

'Are you not afraid?'

'Indeed I am not,' said Lawrence,
and no sooner was the word spoken
than both head and people disappeared,
and he was left in the glen alone by
himself.

He journeyed until he came to
another town, and when he ate and
drank enough, he went out on the
road, and was walking until he came
to a great house on the side of the
road. As the night was closing in, he
went in to try if he could get lodging.

There was a young man at the door who said to him—

'How far are you going, or what are you in search of?'

'I do not know how far I am going, but I am in search of something that will put fear on me,' said Lawrence.

'You have not far to go, then,' said the young man; 'if you stop in that big house on the other side of the road there will be fear put on you before morning, and I'll give you twenty pounds into the bargain.'

'I'll stop in it,' said Lawrence.

The young man went with him, opened the door, and brought him into a large room in the bottom of the house, and said to him, 'Put down fire for yourself and I'll send you plenty to eat and drink.' He put down a fire for himself, and there came a girl to him and brought him everything that he wanted.

He went on very well, until the hour of midnight came, and then he

heard a great sound over his head, and
it was not long until a stallion and a
bull came in and commenced to fight.
Lawrence never put to them nor from
them, and when they were tired fighting they went out. Lawrence went to
sleep, and he never awoke until the
young man came in in the morning,
and he was surprised when he saw
Lawrence alive. He asked him had
he seen anything.

'I saw a stallion and a bull fighting
hard for about two hours,' said Lawrence.

'And weren't you afraid?' said the
young man.

'I was not,' says Lawrence.

'If you wait to-night again, I'll give
you another twenty pounds,' says the
young man.

'I'll wait, and welcome,' says Lawrence.

The second night, about ten o'clock,
Lawrence was going to sleep, when two
black rams came in and began fighting

hard.   Lawrence neither put to them
nor from them, and when twelve
o'clock struck they went out.   The
young man came in the morning and
asked him did he see anything last
night.

'I saw two black rams fighting,' said
Lawrence.

'Were you afraid at all?' said the
young man.

'I was not,' said Lawrence.

'Wait to-night, and I'll give you
another twenty pounds,' says the
young man.

'All right,' says Lawrence.

The third night he was falling
asleep, when there came in a gray old
man and said to him—

'You are the best hero in Ireland; I
died twenty years ago, and all that time
I have been in search of a man like
you.   Come with me now till I show
you your riches; I told you when you
were watching your mother's grave that
there was great riches waiting for you.'

He took Lawrence to a chamber under ground, and showed him a large pot filled with gold, and said to him—

'You will have all that if you give twenty pounds to Mary Kerrigan the widow, and get her forgiveness for me for a wrong I did her. Then buy this house, marry my daughter, and you will be happy and rich as long as you live.'

The next morning the young man came to Lawrence and asked him did he see anything last night.

'I did,' said Lawrence, 'and it's certain that there will be a ghost always in it, but nothing in the world would frighten me; I'll buy the house and the land round it, if you like.'

'I'll ask no price for the house, but I won't part with the land under a thousand pounds, and I'm sure you haven't that much.'

'I have more than would buy all the land and all the herds you have,' said Lawrence.

When the young man heard that Lawrence was so rich, he invited him to come to dinner. Lawrence went with him, and when the dead man's daughter saw him she fell in love with him.

Lawrence went to the house of Mary Kerrigan and gave her twenty pounds, and got her forgiveness for the dead man. Then he married the young man's sister and spent a happy life. He died as he lived, without there being fear on him.

CATS

SEANCHAN THE BARD AND THE KING OF THE CATS

By Lady Wilde

WHEN Seanchan, the renowned Bard, was made *Ard-Filé*, or Chief Poet of Ireland, Guaire, the king of Connaught, to do him honour, made a great feast for him and the whole Bardic Association. And all the professors and learned men went to the king's house, the great ollaves of poetry and history and music, and of the arts and sciences; and the learned, aged females, Grug and Grag and Grangait; and all the chief poets and poetesses of Ireland, an amazing number. But Guaire the king entertained them all splendidly, so that the ancient pathway to his palace is still called 'The Road of the Dishes.'

And each day he asked, 'How fares it with my noble guests?' But they were all discontented, and wanted things he could not get for them. So he was very sorrowful, and prayed to God to be delivered from 'the learned men and women, a vexatious class.'

Still the feast went on for three days and three nights. And they drank and made merry. And the whole Bardic Association entertained the nobles with the choicest music and professional accomplishments.

But Seanchan sulked and would neither eat nor drink, for he was jealous of the nobles of Connaught. And when he saw how much they consumed of the best meats and wine, he declared he would taste no food till they and their servants were all sent away out of the house.

And when Guaire asked him again, 'How fares my noble guest, and this great and excellent people?' Seanchan answered, 'I have never had worse days, nor worse nights, nor worse dinners in my life.' And he ate nothing for three whole days.

Then the king was sorely grieved that the whole Bardic Association should be feasting and drinking while Seanchan, the chief poet of Erin, was fasting and weak. So he sent his favourite serving-man, a person of mild manners and cleanliness, to offer special dishes to the bard.

'Take them away,' said Seanchan; 'I'll have none of them.'

'And why, O Royal Bard?' asked the servitor.

'Because thou art an uncomely youth,' answered Seanchan. 'Thy grandfather was chip-nailed—I have seen him; I shall eat no food from thy hands.'

Then the king called a beautiful maiden to him, his foster - daughter, and said, 'Lady, bring thou this wheaten cake and this dish of salmon to the illustrious poet, and serve him thyself.' So the maiden went.

But when Seanchan saw her he asked: 'Who sent thee hither, and why hast thou brought me food?'

'My lord the king sent me, O Royal Bard,' she answered, 'because I am comely to look upon, and he bade me serve thee with food myself.'

'Take it away,' said Seanchan, 'thou art an unseemly girl, I know of none more ugly. I have seen thy grandmother; she sat on a wall one day and pointed out the way with her hand to some travelling lepers. How could I touch thy food?' So the maiden went away in sorrow.

And then Guaire the king was indeed angry, and he exclaimed, 'My malediction on the mouth that uttered that! May the kiss of a leper be on Seanchan's lips before he dies!'

Now there was a young serving-girl there, and she said to Seanchan, 'There is a hen's egg in the place, my lord, may I bring it to thee, O Chief Bard?'

'It will suffice,' said Seanchan; 'bring it that I may eat.'

But when she went to look for it, behold the egg was gone.

'Thou hast eaten it,' said the bard, in wrath.

'Not so, my lord,' she answered; 'but the mice, the nimble race, have carried it away.'

'Then I will satirise them in a poem,' said Seanchan; and forthwith he chanted so bitter a satire against them that ten mice fell dead at once in his presence.

''Tis well,' said Seanchan; 'but the cat is the one most to blame, for it was her duty to suppress the mice. Therefore I shall satirise the tribe of

L

the cats, and their chief lord, Irusan, son of Arusan; for I know where he lives with his wife Spit-fire, and his daughter Sharp-tooth, with her brothers the Purrer and the Growler. But I shall begin with Irusan himself, for he is king, and answerable for all the cats.'

And he said: 'Irusan, monster of claws, who strikes at the mouse but lets it go; weakest of cats. The otter did well who bit off the tips of thy progenitor's ears, so that every cat since is jagged-eared. Let thy tail hang down; it is right, for the mouse jeers at thee.'

Now Irusan heard these words in his cave, and he said to his daughter Sharp-tooth: 'Seanchan has satirised me, but I will be avenged.'

'Nay, father,' she said, 'bring him here alive that we may all take our revenge.'

'I shall go then and bring him,' said Irusan; 'so send thy brothers after me.

Now when it was told to Seanchan
that the King of the Cats was on his
way to come and kill him, he was
timorous, and besought Guaire and
all the nobles to stand by and protect
him. And before long a vibrating,
impressive, impetuous sound was heard,
like a raging tempest of fire in full
blaze. And when the cat appeared
he seemed to them of the size of a
bullock ; and this was his appearance
— rapacious, panting, jagged - eared,
snub - nosed, sharp - toothed, nimble,
angry, vindictive, glare-eyed, terrible,
sharp-clawed. Such was his similitude.
But he passed on amongst them, not
minding till he came to Seanchan ;
and him he seized by the arm and
jerked him up on his back, and made
off the way he came before any one
could touch him ; for he had no other
object in view but to get hold of the
poet.

Now Seanchan, being in evil plight,
had recourse to flattery. 'O Irusan,'

he exclaimed, 'how truly splendid thou
art: such running, such leaps, such
strength, and such agility! But what
evil have I done, O Irusan, son of
Arusan? spare me, I entreat. I invoke
the saints between thee and me, O
great King of the Cats.'

But not a bit did the cat let go his
hold for all this fine talk, but went
straight on to Clonmacnoise, where
there was a forge; and St. Kieran
happened to be there standing at the
door.

'What!' exclaimed the saint; 'is
that the Chief Bard of Erin on the
back of a cat? Has Guaire's hospitality ended in this?' And he ran for
a red-hot bar of iron that was in the
furnace, and struck the cat on the
side with it, so that the iron passed
through him, and he fell down lifeless.

'Now my curse on the hand that
gave that blow!' said the bard, when
he got upon his feet.

'And wherefore?' asked St. Kieran.

'Because,' answered Seanchan, 'I would rather Irusan had killed me, and eaten me every bit, that so I might bring disgrace on Guaire for the bad food he gave me; for it was all owing to his wretched dinners that I got into this plight.'

And when all the other kings heard of Seanchan's misfortunes, they sent to beg he would visit their courts. But he would have neither kiss nor welcome from them, and went on his way to the bardic mansion, where the best of good living was always to be had. And ever after the kings were afraid to offend Seanchan.

So as long as he lived he had the chief place at the feast, and all the nobles there were made to sit below him, and Seanchan was content. And in time he and Guaire were reconciled; and Seanchan and all the ollaves, and the whole Bardic Association, were feasted by the king for thirty days in noble style, and had the choicest of viands and the best of French wines to drink, served in goblets of silver. And in return for his splendid hospitality the Bardic Association decreed unanimously a vote of thanks to the king. And they praised him in poems as ' Guaire the Generous,' by which name he was ever after known in history, for the words of the poet are immortal.

OWNEY AND OWNEY-NA-PEAK

By Gerald Griffen

WHEN Ireland had kings of her own—when there was no such thing as a coat made of red cloth in the country—when there was plenty in men's houses, and peace and quietness at men's doors (and that is a long time since)—there lived, in a village not far from the great city of Lumneach,[1] two young men, cousins: one of them named Owney, a smart, kind-hearted, handsome youth, with limb of a delicate form, and a very good understanding.

[1] The present Limerick.

His cousin's name was Owney too, and
the neighbours christened him Owney-
na-peak (Owney of the nose), on account of a long nose he had got—a
thing so out of all proportion, that
after looking at one side of his face, it
was a smart morning's walk to get
round the nose and take a view of the
other (at least, so the people used to
say).   He was a stout, able-bodied
fellow, as stupid as a beaten hound,
and he was, moreover, a cruel tyrant
to his young cousin, with whom he
lived in a kind of partnership.

Both of them were of a humble
station.   They were smiths—whitesmiths—and they got a good deal of
business to do from the lords of the
court, and the knights, and all the
grand people of the city.   But one
day young Owney was in town, he saw
a great procession of lords, and ladies,
and generals, and great people, among
whom was the king's daughter of the
court—and surely it is not possible for

the young rose itself to be so beautiful as she was. His heart fainted at her sight, and he went home desperately in love, and not at all disposed to business.

Money, he was told, was the surest way of getting acquainted with the king, and so he began saving until he had put together a few *hogs*,[1] but Owney-na-peak, finding where he had hid them, seized on the whole, as he used to do on all young Owney's earnings.

One evening young Owney's mother found herself about to die, so she called her son to her bedside and said to him: 'You have been a most dutiful good son, and 'tis proper you should be rewarded for it. Take this china cup to the fair,—there is a fairy gift upon it,—use your own wit, look about you, and let the highest bidder have it—and so, my white-headed boy,[2] God bless you!'

---

[1] A *hog*, 1s. 1d.
[2] White-haired boy, a curious Irish phrase for the favourite child.

The young man drew the little bedcurtain down over his dead mother, and in a few days after, with a heavy heart, he took his china cup, and set off to the fair of Garryowen.

The place was merry enough. The field that is called Gallows Green now was covered with tents. There was plenty of wine (poteen not being known in these days, let alone *parliament*), a great many handsome girls, and 'tis unknown all the *keoh* that was with the boys and themselves. Poor Owney walked all the day through the fair, wishing to try his luck, but ashamed to offer his china cup among all the fine things that were there for sale. Evening was drawing on at last, and he was thinking of going home, when a strange man tapped him on the shoulder, and said: 'My good youth, I have been marking you through the fair the whole day, going about with that cup in your hand, speaking to nobody, and looking as if you would be wanting something or another.'

'I'm for selling it,' said Owney.

'What is it you're for selling, you say?' said a second man, coming up, and looking at the cup.

'Why then,' said the first man, 'and what's that to you, for a prying meddler? what do you want to know what it is he's for selling?'

'Bad manners to you (and where's the use of my wishing you what you have already?), haven't I a right to ask the price of what's in the fair?'

'E'then, the knowledge o' the price is all you'll have for it,' says the first. 'Here, my lad, is a golden piece for your cup.'

'That cup shall never hold drink or diet in your house, please Heaven,' says the second; 'here's two gold pieces for the cup, lad.'

'Why then, see this now—if I was forced to fill it to the rim with gold before I could call it mine, you shall never hold that cup between your fingers. Here, boy, do you mind me, give me that, once for all, and here's ten gold pieces for it, and say no more.'

'Ten gold pieces for a china cup!' said a great lord of the court, who just rode up at that minute, 'it must surely be a valuable article. Here, boy, here are twenty pieces for it, and give it to my servant.'

'Give it to mine,' cried another lord of the party, 'and here's my purse, where you will find ten more. And if any man offers another fraction for it to outbid that, I'll spit him on my sword like a snipe.'

'I outbid him,' said a fair young lady in a veil, by his side, flinging twenty golden pieces more on the ground.

There was no voice to outbid the lady, and young Owney, kneeling, gave the cup into her hands.

'Fifty gold pieces for a china cup,' said Owney to himself, as he plodded

on home, 'that was not worth two!
Ah! mother, you knew that vanity had
an open hand.'

But as he drew near home he determined to hide his money somewhere,
knowing, as he well did, that his cousin
would not leave him a single cross to
bless himself with. So he dug a little
pit, and buried all but two pieces,
which he brought to the house. His
cousin, knowing the business on which
he had gone, laughed heartily when he
saw him enter, and asked him what
luck he had got with his punch-bowl.

'Not so bad, neither,' says Owney.
'Two pieces of gold is not a bad price
for an article of old china.'

'Two gold pieces, Owney, honey!
Erra, let us see 'em, maybe you would?'
He took the cash from Owney's hand,
and after opening his eyes in great
astonishment at the sight of so much
money, he put them into his pocket.

'Well, Owney, I'll keep them safe
for you, in my pocket within. But

tell us, maybe you would, how come you to get such a *mort* o' money for an old cup o' painted chaney, that wasn't worth, maybe, a fi'penny bit?'

'To get into the heart o' the fair, then, free and easy, and to look about me, and to cry old china, and the first man that *come* up, he to ask me, what is it I'd be asking for the cup, and I to say out bold: "A hundred pieces of gold," and he to laugh hearty, and we to huxter together till he beat me down to two, and there's the whole way of it all.'

Owney-na-peak made as if he took no note of this, but next morning early he took an old china saucer himself had in his cupboard, and off he set, without saying a word to anybody, to the fair.   You may easily imagine that it created no small surprise in the place when they heard a great big fellow with a china saucer in his hand crying out: 'A raal *chaney* saucer going for a hundred pieces of goold! raal chaney —who'll be buying?'

'Erra, what's that you're saying, you great gomeril?' says a man, coming up to him, and looking first at the saucer and then in his face. 'Is it thinking anybody would go make a *muthaun* of himself to give the like for that saucer?' But Owney-na-peak had no answer to make, only to cry out: 'Raal chaney! one hundred pieces of goold!'

A crowd soon collected about him, and finding he would give no account of himself, they all fell upon him, beat him within an inch of his life, and after having satisfied themselves upon him, they went their way laughing and shouting. Towards sunset he got up, and crawled home as well as he could, without cup or money. As soon as Owney saw him, he helped him into the forge, looking very mournful, although, if the truth must be told, it was to revenge himself for former good deeds of his cousin that he set him about this foolish business.

'Come here, Owney, eroo,' said his cousin, after he had fastened the forge door and heated two irons in the fire. 'You child of mischief!' said he, when he had caught him, 'you shall never see the fruits of your roguery again, for I will put out your eyes.' And so saying he snatched one of the red-hot irons from the fire.

It was all in vain for poor Owney to throw himself on his knees, and ask mercy, and beg and implore forgiveness; he was weak, and Owney-na-peak was strong; he held him fast, and burned out both his eyes. Then taking him, while he was yet fainting from the pain, upon his back, he carried him off to the bleak hill of Knockpatrick,[1] a great distance, and there laid him under a tombstone, and

[1] A hill in the west of the County of Limerick, on the summit of which are the ruins of an old church, with a burying-ground still in use. The situation is exceedingly singular and bleak.

went his ways. In a little time after,
Owney came to himself.

'O sweet light of day! what is to
become of me now?' thought the
poor lad, as he lay on his back under
the tomb. 'Is this to be the fruit of
that unhappy present? Must I be
dark for ever and ever? and am I
never more to look upon that sweet
countenance, that even in my blindness is not entirely shut out from me?'
He would have said a great deal more
in this way, and perhaps more pathetic
still, but just then he heard a great
mewing, as if all the cats in the world
were coming up the hill together in
one faction. He gathered himself up,
and drew back under the stone, and
remained quite still, expecting what
would come next. In a very short
time he heard all the cats purring and
mewing about the yard, whisking over
the tombstones, and playing all sorts of
pranks among the graves. He felt the
tails of one or two brush his nose; and

M

well for him it was that they did not
discover him there, as he afterwards
found.   At last—

'Silence!' said one of the cats,
and they were all as mute as so many
mice in an instant. 'Now, all you
cats of this great county, small and
large, gray, red, yellow, black, brown,
mottled, and white, attend to what I'm
going to tell you in the name of your
king and the master of all the cats.
The sun is down, and the moon is up,
and the night is silent, and no mortal
hears us, and I may tell you a secret.
You know the king of Munster's
daughter?'

'O yes, to be sure, and why wouldn't
we? Go on with your story,' said all
the cats together.

'I have heard of her for one,' said
a little dirty-faced black cat, speaking
after they had all done, 'for I'm the
cat that sits upon the hob of Owney
and Owney-na-peak, the whitesmiths,
and I know many's the time young

Owney does be talking of her, when he sits by the fire alone, rubbing me down and planning how he can get into her father's court.'

'Whist, you natural!' says the cat that was making the speech, 'what do you think we care for your Owney, or Owney-na-peak?'

'Murther, murther!' thinks Owney to himself, 'did anybody ever hear the aiqual of this?'

'Well, gentlemen,' says the cat again, 'what I have to say is this. The king was last week struck with blindness, and you all know well, how and by what means any blindness may be cured. You know there is no disorder that can ail mortal frame, that may not be removed by praying a round at the well of Barrygowen[1]

---

[1] The practice of praying rounds, with the view of healing diseases, at Barrygowen well, in the County of Limerick, is still continued, notwithstanding the exertions of the neighbouring Catholic priesthood, which have diminished, but not abolished it.

yonder, and the king's disorder is such, that no other cure whatever can be had for it. Now, beware, don't let the secret pass one o' yer lips, for there's a great-grandson of Simon Magus, that is coming down to try his skill, and he it is that must use the water and marry the princess, who is to be given to any one so fortunate as to heal her father's eyes; and on that day, gentlemen, we are all promised a feast of the fattest mice that ever walked the ground.' This speech was wonderfully applauded by all the cats, and presently after, the whole crew scampered off, jumping, and mewing, and purring, down the hill.

Owney, being sensible that they were all gone, came from his hiding-place, and knowing the road to Barrygowen well, he set off, and groped his way out, and shortly knew, by the rolling of the waves,[1] coming in from the point of Foynes, that he was near the place.

[1] Of the Shannon.

He got to the well, and making a round like a good Christian, rubbed his eyes with the well-water, and looking up, saw day dawning in the east. Giving thanks, he jumped up on his feet, and you may say that Owney-na-peak was much astonished on opening the door of the forge to find him there, his eyes as well or better than ever, and his face as merry as a dance.

'Well, cousin,' said Owney, smiling, 'you have done me the greatest service that one man can do another; you put me in the way of getting two pieces of gold,' said he, showing two he had taken from his hiding-place. 'If you could only bear the pain of suffering me just to put out your eyes, and lay you in the same place as you laid me, who knows what luck you'd have?'

'No, there's no occasion for putting out eyes at all, but could not you lay me, just as I am, to-night, in that place, and let me try my own fortune, if it be a thing you tell thruth; and what else

could put the eyes in your head, after
I burning them out with the irons?'

'You'll know all that in time,' says
Owney, stopping him in his speech,
for just at that minute, casting his eye
towards the hob, he saw the cat sitting
upon it, and looking very hard at him.
So he made a sign to Owney-na-peak
to be silent, or talk of something else;
at which the cat turned away her eyes,
and began washing her face, quite
simple, with her two paws, looking
now and then sideways into Owney's
face, just like a Christian.   By and by,
when she had walked out of the forge,
he shut the door after her, and finished
what he was going to say, which made
Owney-na-peak still more anxious than
before to be placed under the tombstone.   Owney agreed to it very readily,
and just as they were done speaking,
cast a glance towards the forge window,
where he saw the imp of a cat, just
with her nose and one eye peeping
in through a broken pane.   He said

nothing, however, but prepared to carry his cousin to the place; where, towards nightfall, he laid him as he had been laid himself, snug under the tombstone, and went his way down the hill, resting in Shanagolden that night, to see what would come of it in the morning.

Owney-na-peak had not been more than two or three hours or so lying down, when he heard the very same noises coming up the hill, that had puzzled Owney the night before. Seeing the cats enter the churchyard, he began to grow very uneasy, and strove to hide himself as well as he could, which was tolerably well too, all being covered by the tombstone excepting part of the nose, which was so long that he could not get it to fit by any means. You may say to yourself, that he was not a little surprised, when he saw the cats all assemble like a congregation going to hear mass, some sitting, some walking about, and asking one another after the kittens and the like, and more of them stretching themselves upon the tombstones, and waiting the speech of their commander.

Silence was proclaimed at length, and he spoke: 'Now all you cats of this great county, small and large, gray, red, yellow, black, brown, mottled, or white, attend——'

'Stay! stay!' said a little cat with a dirty face, that just then came running into the yard. 'Be silent, for there are mortal ears listening to what you say. I have run hard and fast to say that your words were overheard last night. I am the cat that sits upon the hob of Owney and Owney-na-peak, and I saw a bottle of the water of Barrygowen hanging up over the chimbley this morning in their house.'

In an instant all the cats began screaming, and mewing, and flying, as if they were mad, about the yard, searching every corner, and peeping under every tombstone. Poor Owney-

na-peak endeavoured as well as he could
to hide himself from them, and began
to thump his breast and cross himself, but it was all in vain, for
one of the cats saw the long nose
peeping from under the stone, and in
a minute they dragged him, roaring
and bawling, into the very middle of
the churchyard, where they flew upon
him all together, and made *smithereens*
of him, from the crown of his head to
the soles of his feet.

The next morning very early, young
Owney came to the churchyard, to see
what had become of his cousin. He
called over and over again upon his
name, but there was no answer given.
At last, entering the place of tombs, he
found his limbs scattered over the earth.

'So that is the way with you, is it?'
said he, clasping his hands, and looking
down on the bloody fragments; 'why
then, though you were no great things
in the way of kindness to me when
your bones were together, that isn't

the reason why I'd be glad to see
them torn asunder this morning early.'
So gathering up all the pieces that he
could find, he put them into a bag he
had with him, and away with him to
the well of Barrygowen, where he lost
no time in making a round, and
throwing them in, all in a heap. In
an instant, he saw Owney-na-peak as
well as ever, scrambling out of the
well, and helping him to get up, he
asked him how he felt himself.

'Oh! is it how I'd feel myself you'd
want to know?' said the other; 'easy
and I'll tell you. Take that for a
specimen!' giving him at the same
time a blow on the head, which you
may say wasn't long in laying Owney
sprawling on the ground. Then without giving him a minute's time to
recover, he thrust him into the very
bag from which he had been just
shaken himself, resolving within himself to drown him in the Shannon at
once, and put an end to him for ever.

Growing weary by the way, he
stopped at a shebeen house *over-
right* Robertstown Castle, to refresh
himself with a *morning*, before he'd
go any farther. Poor Owney did not
know what to do when he came to
himself, if it might be rightly called
coming to himself, and the great bag
tied up about him. His wicked cousin
shot him down behind the door in the
kitchen, and telling him he'd have his
life surely if he stirred, he walked in
to take something that's good in the
little parlour.

Owney could not for the life of him
avoid cutting a hole in the bag, to
have a peep about the kitchen, and
see whether he had no means of escape.
He could see only one person, a simple-
looking man, who was counting his
beads in the chimney-corner, and now
and then striking his breast, and looking up as if he was praying greatly.

'Lord,' says he, 'only give me
death, death, and a favourable judg-

ment! I haven't anybody now to look after, nor anybody to look after me. What's a few tinpennies to save a man from want? Only a quiet grave is all I ask.'

'Murther, murther!' says Owney to himself, 'here's a man wants death and can't have it, and here am I going to have it, and, in troth, I don't want it at all, see.' So, after thinking a little what he had best do, he began to sing out very merrily, but lowering his voice, for fear he should be heard in the next room:

> ' To him that tied me here,
>   Be thanks and praises given!
> I'll bless him night and day,
>   For packing me to heaven.
> Of all the roads you'll name,
>   He surely will not lag,
> Who takes his way to heaven
>   By travelling in a bag!'

'To heaven, *ershishin*?'[1] said the man in the chimney-corner, opening

[1] Does he say?

his mouth and his eyes; 'why then,
you'd be doing a Christian turn, if you'd
take a neighbour with you, that's tired
of this bad and villainous world.'

'You're a fool, you're a fool!' said
Owney.

'I know I am, at least so the
neighbours always tell me—but what
hurt? Maybe I have a Christian soul
as well as another; and fool or no fool,
in a bag or out of a bag, I'd be glad
and happy to go the same road it is
you are talking of.'

After seeming to make a great
favour of it, in order to allure him the
more to the bargain, Owney agreed to
put him into the bag instead of himself;
and cautioning him against saying a
word, he was just going to tie him,
when he was touched with a little
remorse for going to have the innocent
man's life taken: and seeing a slip of
a pig that was killed the day before, in
a corner, hanging up, the thought
struck him that it would do just as

well to put it in the bag in their place. No sooner said than done, to the great surprise of the natural, he popped the pig into the bag and tied it up.

'Now,' says he, 'my good friend, go home, say nothing, but bless the name in heaven for saving your life; and you were as near losing it this morning as ever man was that didn't know.'

They left the house together. Presently out comes Owney-na-peak, very hearty; and being so, he was not able to perceive the difference in the contents of the bag, but hoisting it upon his back, he sallied out of the house. Before he had gone far, he came to the rock of Foynes, from the top of which he flung his burden into the salt waters.

Away he went home, and knocked at the door of the forge, which was opened to him by Owney. You may fancy him to yourself crossing and blessing himself over and over again, when he saw, as he thought, the ghost

standing before him. But Owney
looked very merry, and told him not
to be afraid. 'You did many is the
•good turn in your life,' says he, 'but
the equal of this never.' So he up
and told him that he found the finest
place in the world at the bottom of the
waters, and plenty of money. 'See
these four pieces for a specimen,'
showing him some he had taken from
his own hiding hole: 'what do you
think of that for a story?'

'Why then that it's a droll one, no
less; sorrow bit av I wouldn't have a
mind to try my luck in the same way;
how did you come home here before
me that took the straight road, and
didn't stop for so much as my *gusthah*[1]
since I left Knockpatrick?'

'Oh, there's a short cut under the
waters,' said Owney. 'Mind and only
be civil while you're in Thiernaoge,[2]
and you'll make a sight o' money.'

---

[1] Literally—*walk in.*
[2] The abode of the fairies.

Well became Owney, he thrust his cousin into the bag, tied it about him, and putting it into a car that was returning after leaving a load of oats. at a corn-store in the city, it was not long before he was at Foynes again. Here he dismounted, and going to the rock, he was, I am afraid, half inclined to start his burden into the wide water, when he saw a small skiff making towards the point. He hailed her, and learned that she was about to board a great vessel from foreign parts, that was sailing out of the river. So he went with his bag on board, and making his bargain with the captain of the ship, he left Owney-na-peak along with the crew, and never was troubled with him after, from that day to this.

As he was passing by Barrygowen well, he filled a bottle with the water; and going home, he bought a fine suit of clothes with the rest of the money he had buried, and away he set off in the morning to the city of

Lumneach. He walked through the town, admiring everything he saw, until he came before the palace of the king. Over the gates of this he saw a number of spikes, with a head of a man stuck upon each, grinning in the sunshine.

Not at all daunted, he knocked very boldly at the gate, which was opened by one of the guards of the palace. 'Well! who are you, friend?'

'I am a great doctor that's come from foreign parts to cure the king's eyesight. Lead me to his presence this minute.'

'Fair and softly,' said the soldier. 'Do you see all those heads that are stuck up there? Yours is very likely to be keeping company by them, if you are so foolish as to come inside these walls. They are the heads of all the doctors in the land who came before you; and that's what makes the town so fine and healthy this time past, praised be Heaven for the same!'

N

'Don't be talking, you great gomeril,' says Owney; 'only bring me to the king at once.'

He was brought before the king. After being warned of his fate if he should fail to do all that he undertook, the place was made clear of all but a few guards, and Owney was informed once more, that if he should restore the king's eyes, he should wed with the princess, and have the crown after her father's death. This put him in great spirits, and after making a round upon his bare knees about the bottle, he took a little of the water, and rubbed it into the king's eyes. In a minute he jumped up from his throne and looked about him as well as ever. He ordered Owney to be dressed out like a king's son, and sent word to his daughter that she should receive him that instant for her husband.

You may say to yourself that the princess, glad as she was of her father's recovery, did not like this message.

Small blame to her, when it is considered that she never set her eyes
upon the man himself. However, her
mind was changed wonderfully when
he was brought before her, covered
with gold and diamonds, and all sorts
of grand things. Wishing, however,
to know whether he had as good a
wit as he had a person, she told him
that he should give her, on the next
morning, an answer to two questions,
otherwise she would not hold him
worthy of her hand. Owney bowed,
and she put the questions as follows :

'What is that which is the sweetest
thing in the world?'

'What are the three most beautiful
objects in the creation?'

These were puzzling questions; but
Owney having a small share of brains
of his own, was not long in forming
an opinion upon the matter. He was
very impatient for the morning; but
it came just as slow and regular as if
he were not in the world. In a short

time he was summoned to the courtyard, where all the nobles of the land
assembled, with flags waving, and
trumpets sounding, and all manner of
glorious doings going on.   The princess
was placed on a throne of gold near
her father, and there was a beautiful
carpet spread for Owney to stand
upon while he answered her questions.
After the trumpets were silenced, she
put the first, with a clear sweet voice,
and he replied:

'It's salt!' says he, very stout, out.

There was a great applause at the
answer; and the princess owned,
smiling, that he had judged right.

'But now,' said she, 'for the second.
What are the three most beautiful
things in the creation?'

'Why,' answered the young man,
'here they are.   A ship in full sail—
a field of wheat in ear—and——'

What the third most beautiful thing
was, all the people didn't hear; but
there was a great blushing and laughing

among the ladies, and the princess smiled and nodded at him, quite pleased with his wit. Indeed, many said that the judges of the land themselves could not have answered better, had they been in Owney's place; nor could there be anywhere found a more likely or well-spoken young man. He was brought first to the king, who took him in his arms, and presented him to the princess. She could not help acknowledging to herself that his understanding was quite worthy of his handsome person. Orders being immediately given for the marriage to proceed, they were made one with all speed; and it is said, that before another year came round, the fair princess was one of the most beautiful objects in the creation.

KINGS AND WARRIORS

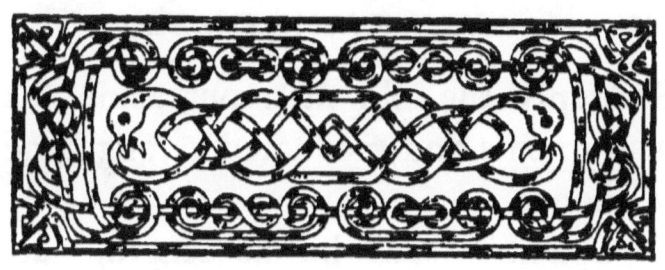

THE
KNIGHTING OF CUCULAIN [1]

By Standish O'Grady

NE night in the month of the fires of Bel, Cathvah, the Druid and star-gazer, was observing the heavens through his astrological instruments. Beside him was Cuculain, just then completing his sixteenth year. Since the exile of Fergus MacRoy, Cuculain had attached himself most to the Ard-Druid, and delighted to be along with him in his studies and observations.

[1] Cuculain was the great hero of legendary Ireland.

Suddenly the old man put aside his instruments and meditated a long time in silence.

'Setanta,' said he at length, 'art thou yet sixteen years of age?'

'No, father,' replied the boy.

'It will then be difficult to persuade the king to knight thee and enrol thee among his knights,' said Cathvah. 'Yet this must be done to-morrow, for it has been revealed to me that he whom Concobar MacNessa shall present with arms to-morrow, will be renowned to the most distant ages, and to the ends of the earth. Thou shalt be presented with arms to-morrow, and after that thou mayest retire for a season among thy comrades, nor go out among the warriors until thy strength is mature.'

The next day Cathvah procured the king's consent to the knighting of Cuculain. Now on the same morning, one of his grooms came to Concobar MacNessa and said: 'O chief of the

Red Branch, thou knowest how no horse has eaten barley, or ever occupied the stall where stood the divine steed which, with another of mortal breed, in the days of Kimbay MacFiontann, was accustomed to bear forth to the battle the great war-queen, Macha Monga-Rue; but ever since that stall has been empty, and no mortal steed hath profaned the stall in which the deathless Lia Macha was wont to stand. Yet, O Concobar, as I passed into the great stables on the east side of the courtyard, wherein are the steeds of thy own ambus, and in which is that spot since held sacred, I saw in the empty stall a mare, gray almost to whiteness, and of a size and beauty such as I have never seen, who turned to look upon me as I entered the stable, having very gentle eyes, but such as terrified me, so that I let fall the vessel in which I was bearing curds for the steed of Konaul Clareena; and she approached me, and laid her head upon my shoulder, making a strange noise.'

Now as the groom was thus speaking, Cowshra Mend Macha, a younger son of Concobar, came before the king, and said: 'Thou knowest, O my father, that house in which is preserved the chariot of Kimbay MacFiontann, wherein he and she, whose name I bear, the great queen that protects our nation, rode forth to the wars in the ancient days, and how it has been preserved ever since, and that it is under my care to keep bright and clean. Now this day at sunrise I approached the house, as is my custom, and approaching, I heard dire voices, clamorous and terrible, that came from within, and noises like the noise of battle, and shouts as of warriors in the agony of the conflict, that raise their voices with short intense cries as they ply their weapons, avoiding or inflicting death. Then I went back terrified, but there met me Minrowar,

son of Gerkin, for he came but last
night from Moharne, in the east, and
he went to look at his own steeds;
but together we opened the gate of
the chariot-house, and the bronze of
the chariot burned like glowing fire,
and the voices cried out in acclaim,
when we stood in the doorway, and
the light streamed into the dark
chamber. Doubtless, a great warrior
will appear amongst the Red Branch,
for men say that not for a hundred
years have these voices been heard,
and I know not for whom Macha
sends these portents, if it be not for
the son of Sualtam, though he is not
yet of an age to bear arms.'

Thus was Concobar prepared for
the knighting of Cuculain.

Then in the presence of his court,
and his warriors, and the youths who
were the comrades and companions
of Cuculain, Concobar presented the
young hero with his weapons of war,
after he had taken the vows of the

Red Branch, and having also bound himself by certain gæsa.[1] But Cuculain looked narrowly upon the weapons, and he struck the spears together and clashed the sword upon the shield, and he brake the spears in pieces, and the sword, and made chasms in the shield.

'These are not good weapons, O my King,' said the boy.

Then the king presented him with others that were larger and stronger, and these too the boy brake into little pieces.

'These are still worse, O son of Nessa,' said the boy, 'and it is not seemly, O chief of the Red Branch, that on the day that I am to receive my arms I should be made a laughing-stock before the Clanna Rury, being yet but a boy.'

But Concobar MacNessa exulted exceedingly when he beheld the amaz-

---

[1] Curious vows taken by the ancient warriors. Hardly anything definite is known of them. —ED.

ing strength and the waywardness of
the boy, and beneath delicate brows
his eyes glittered like gleaming swords
as he glanced rapidly round on the
crowd of martial men that surrounded
him ; but amongst them all he seemed
himself a bright torch of valour and
war, more pure and clear than polished
steel. But he beckoned to one of
his knights, who hastened away and
returned, bringing Concobar's own
shield and spears and the sword out
of the Tayta Brac, where they were
kept, an equipment in reserve. And
Cuculain shook them and bent them,
and clashed them together, but they
held firm.

'These are good arms, O son of
Nessa,' said Cuculain.

Then there were led forward a pair
of noble steeds and a war-car, and
the king conferred them on Cuculain.
Then Cuculain sprang into the chariot,
and standing with legs apart, he stamped
from side to side, and shook and shook,

and jolted the car until the axle brake and the car itself was broken in pieces.

'This is not a good chariot, O my King,' said the boy.

Then there were led forward three chariots, and all these he brake in succession.

'These are not good chariots, O chief of the Red Branch,' said Cuculain. 'No brave warrior would enter the battle or fight from such rotten foothold.'

Then the king called to his son Cowshra Mead Macha and bade him take Læg, and harness to the war-chariot, of which he had the care, the wondrous gray steed, and that one which had been given him by Kelkar, the son of Uther, and to give Læg a charioteering equipment, to be charioteers of Cuculain. For now it was apparent to all the nobles and to the king that a lion of war had appeared amongst them, and that it was for him Macha had sent these omens.

Then Cuculain's heart leaped in his

breast when he heard the thunder of
the great war-car and the mad whinny-
ing of the horses that smelt the battle
afar. Soon he beheld them with his
eyes, and the charioteer with the golden
fillet of his office, erect in the car,
struggling to subdue their fury. A
gray, long-maned steed, whale-bellied,
broad-chested, behind one yoke; a
black, ugly-maned steed behind the
other.

Like a hawk swooping along the
face of a cliff when the wind is high,
or like the rush of the March wind
over the plain, or like the fleetness of
the stag roused from his lair by the
hounds and covering his first field,
was the rush of those steeds when they
had broken through the restraint of
the charioteer, as though they galloped
over fiery flags, so that the earth shook
and trembled with the velocity of their
motion, and all the time the great car
brayed and shrieked as the wheels of
solid and glittering bronze went round,

o

for there were demons that had their abode in that car.

The charioteer restrained the steeds before the assembly, but nay-the-less a deep pur, like the pur of a tiger, proceeded from the axle. Then the whole assembly lifted up their voices and shouted for Cuculain, and he himself, Cuculain the son of Sualtam, sprang into his chariot, all armed, with a cry as of a warrior springing into his chariot in the battle, and he stood erect and brandished his spears, and the war-sprites of the Gæil shouted along with them, to the Bocanahs and Bananahs and the Genitii Glindi, the wild people of the glens, and the demons of the air, roared around him, when first the great warrior of the Gæil, his battle-arms in his hands, stood equipped for war in his chariot before all the warriors of his tribe, the kings of the Clanna Rury, and the people of Emain Macha.

THE LITTLE WEAVER OF DULEEK GATE

By Samuel Lover

YOU see, there was a waiver lived, wanst upon a time, in Duleek here, hard by the gate, and a very honest, industherous man he was, by all accounts. He had a wife, and av coorse they had childhre, and small blame to them, and plenty of them, so that the poor little waiver was obleeged to work his fingers to the bone a'most to get them the bit and the sup; but he didn't begridge that, for he was an industherous craythur, as I said before, and it was up airly and down late with him, and the loom never standin' still. Well, it was one mornin' that his wife called to him, and he sitting very busy throwin' the shuttle ; and says she, 'Come here,' says she, 'jewel, and ate your brekquest, now that it's ready.' But he never minded her, but wint an workin'.   So in a minit or two more, says she, callin' out to him agin, 'Arrah, lave off slavin' yourself, my darlin', and ate your bit o' brekquest while it is hot.'

'Lave me alone,' says he, and he dhruv the shuttle fasther nor before.

Well, in a little time more, she goes over to him where he sot, and says she, coaxin' him like, 'Thady, dear,' says she, 'the stirabout will be stone cowld if you don't give over that weary work and come and ate it at wanst.'

'I'm busy with a patthern here that is brakin' my heart,' says the waiver ; 'and antil I complate it and masther it intirely I won't quit.'

'Oh, think o' the iligant stirabout, that 'ill be spylte intirely.'

'To the divil with the stirabout,' says he.

'God forgive you,' says she, 'for cursin' your good brekquest.'

'Ay, and you too,' says he.

'Throth, you're as cross as two sticks this blessed morning, Thady,' says the poor wife; 'and it's a heavy handful I have of you when you are cruked in your temper; but stay there if you like, and let your stirabout grow cowld, and not a one o' me 'ill ax you agin;' and with that off she wint, and the waiver, sure enough, was mighty crabbed, and the more the wife spoke to him the worse he got, which, you know, is only nath'ral. Well, he left the loom at last, and wint over to the stirabout, and what would you think but whin he looked at it, it was as black as a crow; for, you see, it was in the hoighth o' summer, and the flies lit upon it to that degree that the stirabout was fairly covered with them.

'Why, thin, bad luck to your impidence,' says the waiver; 'would no place sarve you but that? and is it spyling my brekquest yiz are, you dirty bastes?' And with that, bein' altogether cruked-tempered at the time, he lifted his hand, and he made one great slam at the dish o' stirabout, and killed no less than three score and tin flies at the one blow. It was three score and tin exactly, for he counted the carcasses one by one, and laid them out on a clane plate, for to view them.

Well, he felt a powerful sperit risin' in him, when he seen the slaughther he done, at one blow; and with that he got as consaited as the very dickens, and not a sthroke more work he'd do that day, but out he wint, and was fractious and impident to every one he met, and was squarin' up into their faces and sayin', 'Look at that fist!

that's the fist that killed three score and tin at one blow—Whoo !'

With that all the neighbours thought he was crack'd, and faith, the poor wife herself thought the same when he kem home in the evenin', afther spendin' every rap he had in dhrink, and swaggerin' about the place, and lookin' at his hand every minit.

'Indeed, an' your hand is very dirty, sure enough, Thady jewel,' says the poor wife ; and thrue for her, for he rowled into a ditch comin' home. 'You had betther wash it, darlin'.'

'How dar' you say dirty to the greatest hand in Ireland?' says he, going to bate her.

'Well, it's nat dirty,' says she.

'It is throwin' away my time I have been all my life,' says he ; 'livin' with you at all, and stuck at a loom, nothin' but a poor waiver, when it is Saint George or the Dhraggin I ought to be, which is two of the siven champions o' Christendom.'

'Well, suppose they christened him twice as much,' says the wife; 'sure, what's that to uz?'

'Don't put in your prate,' says he; 'you ignorant sthrap,' says he. 'You're vulgar, woman—you're vulgar—mighty vulgar; but I'll have nothin' more to say to any dirty snakin' thrade again—divil a more waivin' I'll do.'

'Oh, Thady dear, and what'll the children do then?'

'Let them go play marvels,' says he.

'That would be but poor feedin' for them, Thady.'

'They shan't want for feedin',' says he; 'for it's a rich man I'll be soon, and a great man too.'

'Usha, but I'm glad to hear it, darlin',—though I dunna how it's to be, but I think you had betther go to bed, Thady.'

'Don't talk to me of any bed but the bed o' glory, woman,' says he, lookin' mortial grand.

'Oh! God send we'll all be in glory

yet,' says the wife, crassin' herself; 'but go to sleep, Thady, for this present.'

'I'll sleep with the brave yit,' says he.

'Indeed, an' a brave sleep will do you a power o' good, my darlin',' says she.

'And it's I that will be the knight !' says he.

'All night, if you plaze, Thady,' says she.

'None o' your coaxin',' says he. 'I'm determined on it, and I'll set off immediantly, and be a knight arriant.'

'A what ?' says she.

'A knight arriant, woman.'

'Lord, be good to me, what's that ?' says she.

'A knight arriant is a rale gintleman,' says he; 'going round the world for sport, with a swoord by his side, takin' whatever he plazes for himself; and that's a knight arriant,' says he.

Well, sure enough he wint about among his neighbours the next day, and

he got an owld kittle from one, and a
saucepan from another; and he took
them to the tailor, and he sewed him
up a shuit o' tin clothes like any knight
arriant and he borrowed a pot lid, and
that he was very partic'lar about, bekase
it was his shield and he wint to a frind o'
his, a painther and glazier, and made him
paint an his shield in big letthers—

' I'M THE MAN OF ALL MIN,
THAT KILL'D THREE SCORE AND TIN
AT A BLOW.'

'When the people sees *that*,' says
the waiver to himself, 'the sorra one
will dar' for to come near me.'

And with that he towld the wife to
scour out the small iron pot for him,
'For,' says he, 'it will make an iligant
helmet'; and when it was done, he put
it an his head, and his wife said, 'Oh,
murther, Thady jewel, is it puttin' a
great heavy iron pot an your head you
are, by way iv a hat?'

'Sartinly,' says he; 'for a knight

arraint should always have *a woight an his brain.*'

'But, Thady dear,' says the wife, 'there's a hole in it, and it can't keep out the weather.'

'It will be the cooler,' says he, puttin' it an him; 'besides, if I don't like it, it is aisy to stop it with a wisp o' sthraw, or the like o' that.'

'The three legs of it looks mighty quare, stickin' up,' says she.

'Every helmet has a spike stickin' out o' the top of it,' says the waiver; 'and if mine has three, it's only the grandher it is.'

'Well,' says the wife, getting bitther at last, 'all I can say is, it isn't the first sheep's head was dhress'd in it.'

'*Your sarvint, ma'am,*' says he; and off he set.

Well, he was in want of a horse, and so he wint to a field hard by, where the miller's horse was grazin', that used to carry the ground corn round the counthry.

'This is the idintical horse for me,'
says the waiver; 'he is used to carryin'
flour and male, and what am I but
the *flower* o' shovelry in a coat o' *mail*;
so that the horse won't be put out iv
his way in the laste.'

But as he was ridin' him out o' the field,
who should see him but the miller.

'Is it stalin' my horse you are, honest
man?' says the miller.

'No,' says the waiver; 'I'm only
goin' to *ax*ercise him,' says he, 'in the
cool o' the evenin'; it will be good for
his health.'

'Thank you kindly,' says the miller;
'but lave him where he is, and you'll
obleege me.'

'I can't afford it,' says the waiver,
runnin' the horse at the ditch.

'Bad luck to your impidence,' says
the miller; 'you've as much tin about
you as a thravellin' tinker, but you've
more brass.   Come back here, you
vagabone,' says he.

But he was too late; away galloped

the waiver, and took the road to Dublin,
for he thought the best thing he could
do was to go to the King o' Dublin
(for Dublin was a grate place thin, and
had a king iv its own), and he thought,
maybe, the King o' Dublin would give
him work. Well, he was four days
goin' to Dublin, for the baste was not
the best and the roads worse, not all
as one as now; but there was no
turnpikes then, glory be to God ! When
he got to Dublin, he wint sthrait to the
palace, and whin he got into the
coortyard he let his horse go and graze
about the place, for the grass was
growin' out betune the stones ; everything was flourishin' thin in Dublin,
you see. Well, the king was lookin'
out of his dhrawin'-room windy, for
divarshin, whin the waiver kem in ;
but the waiver pretended not to see
him, and he wint over to a stone sate,
undher the windy—for, you see, there
was stone sates all round about the
place for the accommodation o' the

people—for the king was a dacent, obleeging man; well, as I said, the waiver wint over and lay down an one o' the sates, just undher the king's windy, and purtended to go asleep; but he took care to turn out the front of his shield that had the letthers an it; well, my dear, with that, the king calls out to one of the lords of his coort that was standin' behind him, howldin' up the skirt of his coat, accordin' to rayson, and says he : ' Look here,' says he, 'what do you think of a vagabone like that comin' undher my very nose to go sleep?   It is thrue I'm a good king,' says he, 'and I 'commodate the people by havin' sates for them to sit down and enjoy the raycreation and contimplation of seein' me here, lookin' out a' my dhrawin'-room windy, for divarshin; but that is no rayson they are to *make a hotel* o' the place, and come and sleep here.   Who is it at all?' says the king.

'Not a one o' me knows, plaze your majesty.'

'I think he must be a furriner,' says the king; 'bekase his dhress is out-landish.'

'And doesn't know manners, more betoken,' says the lord.

'I'll go down and *circumspect* him myself,' says the king; 'folly me,' says he to the lord, wavin' his hand at the same time in the most dignacious manner.

Down he wint accordingly, followed by the lord; and whin he wint over to where the waiver was lying, sure the first thing he seen was his shield with the big letthers an it, and with that, says he to the lord, 'Bedad,' says he, 'this is the very man I want.'

'For what, plaze your majesty?' says the lord.

'To kill that vagabone dragghin, to be sure,' says the king.

'Sure, do you think he could kill him,' says the lord, 'when all the stoutest knights in the land wasn't aiquil to it, but never kem back, and was ate up alive by the cruel desaiver.'

'Sure, don't you see there,' says the king, pointin' at the shield, 'that he killed three score and tin at one blow? and the man that done *that*, I think, is a match for anything.'

So, with that, he wint over to the waiver and shuck him by the shouldher for to wake him, and the waiver rubbed his eyes as if just wakened, and the king says to him, 'God save you,' said he.

'God save you kindly,' says the waiver, *purtendin'* he was quite onknowst who he was spakin' to.

'Do you know who I am,' says the king, 'that you make so free, good man?'

'No, indeed,' says the waiver; 'you have the advantage o' me.'

'To be sure I have,' says the king, *moighty high*; 'sure, ain't I the King o' Dublin?' says he.

The waiver dhropped down an his two knees forninst the king, and says he, 'I beg God's pardon and yours for the liberty I tuk; plaze your holiness, I hope you'll excuse it.'

'No offince,' says the king; 'get up, good man. And what brings you here?' says he.

'I'm in want o' work, plaze your riverence,' says the waiver.

'Well, suppose I give you work?' says the king.

'I'll be proud to sarve you, my lord,' says the waiver.

'Very well,' says the king. 'You killed three score and tin at one blow, I understan',' says the king.

'Yis,' says the waiver; 'that was the last thrifle o' work I done, and I'm afeard my hand 'll go out o' practice if I don't get some job to do at wanst.'

'You shall have a job immediantly,' says the king. 'It is not three score and tin or any fine thing like that; it is only a blaguard dhraggin that

P

is disturbin' the counthry and ruinatin' my tinanthry wid aitin' their powlthry, and I'm lost for want of eggs,' says the king.

'Throth, thin, plaze your worship,' says the waiver, 'you look as yollow as if you swallowed twelve yolks this minit.'

'Well, I want this dhraggin to be killed,' says the king.   'It will be no throuble in life to you ; and I am only sorry that it isn't betther worth your while, for he isn't worth fearin' at all ; only I must tell you, that he lives in the County Galway, in the middle of a bog, and he has an advantage in that.'

'Oh, I don't value it in the laste,' says the waiver ; 'for the last three score and tin I killed was in a *soft place.*'

'When will you undhertake the job, then ?' says the king.

'Let me at him at wanst,' says the waiver.

'That's what I like,' says the king;

'you're the very man for my money,'
says he.

'Talkin' of money,' says the waiver;
'by the same token, I'll want a thrifle
o' change from you for my thravellin'
charges.'

'As much as you plaze,' says the
king; and with the word, he brought
him into his closet, where there was
an owld stockin' in an oak chest,
burstin' wid goolden guineas.

'Take as many as you plaze,' says
the king; and sure enough, my dear,
the little waiver stuffed his tin clothes
as full as they could howld with them.

'Now, I'm ready for the road,' says
the waiver.

'Very well,' says the king; 'but you
must have a fresh horse,' says he.

'With all my heart,' says the waiver,
who thought he might as well exchange the miller's owld garron for a
betther.

And maybe it's wondherin' you are
that the waiver would think of goin' to

fight the dhraggin afther what he heerd
about him, when he was purtendin' to
be asleep, but he had no sitch notion;
all he intended was,—to fob the goold,
and ride back again to Duleek with his
gains and a good horse. But, you see,
cute as the waiver was, the king was
cuter still; for these high quolity, you
see, is great desaivers; and so the
horse the waiver was put an was larned
on purpose; and sure, the minit he
was mounted, away powdhered the
horse, and the divil a toe he'd go but
right down to Galway. Well, for four
days he was goin' evermore, until at
last the waiver seen a crowd o' people
runnin' as if owld Nick was at their
heels, and they shoutin' a thousand
murdhers and cryin', 'The dhraggin,
the dhraggin!' and he couldn't stop
the horse nor make him turn back, but
away he pelted right forninst the
terrible baste that was comin' up to
him, and there was the most *nefaarious*
smell o' sulphur, savin' your presence,

enough to knock you down; and, faith
the waiver seen he had no time to lose,
and so he threw himself off the horse
and made to a 'three that was growin'
nigh hand, and away he clambered up
into it as nimble as a cat; and not a
minit had he to spare, for the dhraggin
kem up in a powerful rage, and he
devoured the horse body and bones,
in less than no time; and then he
began to sniffle and scent about for the
waiver, and at last he clapt his eye an
him, where he was, up in the three, and
says he, 'In throth, you might as well
come down out o' that,' says he; 'for
I'll have you as sure as eggs is mate.'

'Divil a fut I'll go down,' says the
waiver.

'Sorra care, I care,' says the dhraggin; 'for you're as good as ready
money in my pocket this minit, for
I'll lie undher this three,' says he, 'and
sooner or later you must fall to my
share'; and sure enough he sot down,
and began to pick his teeth with his

tail, afther the heavy brekquest he
made that mornin' (for he ate a whole
village, let alone the horse), and he got
dhrowsy at last, and fell asleep; but
before he wint to sleep, he wound himself all round about the three, all as one
as a lady windin' ribbon round her
finger, so that the waiver could not
escape.

Well, as soon as the waiver knew he
was dead asleep, by the snorin' of him
—and every snore he let out of him
was like a clap o' thunder—that minit
the waiver began to creep down the
three, as cautious as a fox; and he was
very nigh hand the bottom, when, bad
cess to it, a thievin' branch he was
dipindin' an bruk, and down he fell
right a-top o' the dhraggin; but if he
did, good luck was an his side, for
where should he fall but with his two
legs right acrass the dhraggin's neck,
and, my jew'l, he laid howlt o' the
baste's ears, and there he kept his grip,
for the dhraggin wakened and en-

dayvoured for to bite him; but, you
see, by rayson the waiver was behind
his ears, he could not come at him,
and, with that, he endayvoured for to
shake him off; but the divil a stir
could he stir the waiver; and though
he shuk all the scales an his body, he
could not turn the scale agin the
waiver.

'By the hokey, this is too bad
intirely,' says the dhraggin; 'but if
you won't let go,' says he, 'by the
powers o' wildfire, I'll give you a ride
that 'ill astonish your siven small sinses,
my boy'; and, with that, away he flew
like mad; and where do you think he
did fly?—bedad, he flew sthraight for
Dublin, divil a less. But the waiver
bein' an his neck was a great disthress
to him, and he would rather have had
him an *inside passenger*; but, anyway,
he flew and he flew till he kem *slap* up
agin the palace o' the king; for, bein'
blind with the rage, he never seen it,
and he knocked his brains out—that

is, the small thrifle he had—and down
he fell spacheless. An' you see, good
luck would have it, that the King o'
Dublin was lookin' out iv' his dhrawin'-
room windy, for divarshin, that day
also, and whin he seen the waiver
ridin' an the fiery dhraggin (for he was
blazin' like a tar-barrel), he called out
to his coortyers to come and see the
show. 'By the powdhers o' war, here
comes the knight arriant,' says the
king, 'ridin' the dhraggin that's all
afire, and if he gets *into the palace*, yiz
must be ready wid the *fire ingines*,'
says he, 'for to *put him out*.' But
when they seen the dhraggin fall outside, they all run down-stairs and
scampered into the palace-yard for to
circumspect the *curosity*; and by the
time they got down, the waiver had got
off o' the dhraggin's neck, and runnin'
up to the king, says he, 'Plaze your
holiness,' says he, 'I did not think
myself worthy of killin' this facetious
baste, so I brought him to yourself for

to do him the honour of decripitation by your own royal five fingers. But I tamed him first, before I allowed him the liberty for to *dar'* to appear in your royal prisince, and you'll oblige me if you'll just make your mark with your own hand upon the onruly baste's neck.' And with that the king, sure enough, dhrew out his swoord and took the head aff the *dirty* brute as *clane* as a new pin. Well, there was great rejoicin' in the coort that the dhraggin was killed; and says the king to the little waiver, says he, 'You are a knight arriant as it is, and so it would be of no use for to knight you over agin; but I will make you a lord,' says he.

'O Lord!' says the waiver, thunder-struck like at his own good luck.

'I will,' says the king; 'and as you are the first man I ever heer'd tell of that rode a dhraggin, you shall be called Lord *Mount* Dhraggin,' says he.

'And where's my estates, plaze your

holiness?' says the waiver, who always had a sharp look-out afther the main chance.

'Oh, I didn't forget that,' says the king; 'it is my royal pleasure to provide well for you, and for that rayson I make you a present of all the dhraggins in the world, and give you power over them from this out,' says he.

'Is that all?' says the waiver.

'All!' says the king. 'Why, you ongrateful little vagabone, was the like ever given to any man before?'

'I b'lieve not, indeed,' says the waiver; 'many thanks to your majesty.'

'But that is not all I'll do for you,' says the king; 'I'll give you my daughther too in marriage,' says he. Now, you see, that was nothin' more than what he promised the waiver in his first promise; for, by all accounts, the king's daughther was the greatest dhraggin ever was seen, and had the divil's own tongue, and a beard a yard

long, which she *purtended* was put an
her by way of a penance by Father
Mulcahy, her confissor; but it was
well known it was in the family for
ages, and no wondher it was so long,
by rayson of that same.

APPENDIX

CLASSIFICATION OF
IRISH FAIRIES

IRISH Fairies divide themselves into two great classes: the sociable and the solitary. The first are in the main kindly, and the second full of all uncharitableness.

THE SOCIABLE FAIRIES

These creatures, who go about in troops, and quarrel, and make love, much as men and women do, are divided into land fairies or Sheoques (Ir. *Sidheog*, 'a little fairy,') and water fairies or Merrows (Ir. *Moruadh*, 'a sea maid'; the masculine is unknown). At the same time I am

inclined to think that the term Sheoque
may be applied to both upon occasion,
for I have heard of a whole village
turning out to hear two red-capped
water fairies, who were very 'little fairies'
indeed, play upon the bagpipes.

1. *The Sheoques.* — The Sheoques
proper, however, are the spirits that
haunt the sacred thorn bushes and the
green raths.   All over Ireland are little
fields circled by ditches, and supposed to
be ancient fortifications and sheepfolds.
These are the raths, or forts, or 'royalties,'
as they are variously called.   Here,
marrying and giving in marriage, live
the land fairies.   Many a mortal they
are said to have enticed down into their
dim world.   Many more have listened to
their fairy music, till all human cares
and joys drifted from their hearts and
they became great peasant seers or 'Fairy
Doctors,' or great peasant musicians or
poets like Carolan, who gathered his
tunes while sleeping on a fairy rath ; or
else they died in a year and a day, to live
ever after among the fairies.   These
Sheoques are on the whole good ; but

one most malicious habit have they—
a habit worthy of a witch. They steal
children and leave a withered fairy, a
thousand or maybe two thousand years
old, instead. Three or four years ago a
man wrote to one of the Irish papers,
telling of a case in his own village, and
how the parish priest made the fairies
deliver the stolen child up again. At
times full-grown men and women have
been   taken.   Near   the   village   of
Coloney, Sligo, I have been told, lives an
old woman who was taken in her youth.
When she came home at the end of
seven years she had no toes, for she had
danced them off. Now and then one hears
of some real injury being done a person
by the land fairies, but then it is nearly
always deserved. They are said to have
killed two people in the last six months
in the County Down district where I am
now staying. But then these persons
had torn up thorn bushes belonging to
the Sheoques.

2. *The Merrows.*—These water fairies
are said to be common. I asked a
peasant woman once whether the fisher-

men of her village had ever seen one. 'Indeed, they don't like to see them at all,' she answered, 'for they always bring bad weather.' Sometimes the Merrows come out of the sea in the shape of little hornless cows. When in their own shape, they have fishes' tails and wear a red cap called in Irish *cohuleen driuth* (p. 79). The men among them have, according to Croker, green teeth, green hair, pigs' eyes, and red noses; but their women are beautiful, and sometimes prefer handsome fishermen to their green-haired lovers. Near Bantry, in the last century, lived a woman covered with scales like a fish, who was descended, as the story goes, from such a marriage. I have myself never heard tell of this grotesque appearance of the male Merrows, and think it probably a merely local Munster tradition.

THE SOLITARY FAIRIES

These are nearly all gloomy and terrible in some way. There are, however, some among them who have light hearts and brave attire.

1. *The Lepricaun* (Ir. *Leith bhrogan, i.e.* the one shoe maker).—This creature is seen sitting under a hedge mending a shoe, and one who catches him can make him deliver up his crocks of gold, for he is a miser of great wealth ; but if you take your eyes off him the creature vanishes like smoke. He is said to be the child of an evil spirit and a debased fairy, and wears, according to McAnally, a red coat with seven buttons in each row, and a cocked-hat, on the point of which he sometimes spins like a top. In Donegal he goes clad in a great frieze coat.

2. *The Cluricaun* (Ir. *Clobhair-cean* in O'Kearney).—Some writers consider this to be another name for the Lepricaun, given him when he has laid aside his shoe-making at night and goes on the spree. The Cluricauns' occupations are robbing wine-cellars and riding sheep and shepherds' dogs for a livelong night, until the morning finds them panting and mud-covered.

3. *The Gonconer or Ganconagh* (Ir.

Gean-canogh, i.e. love-talker).—This is a
creature of the Lepricaun type, but, unlike
him, is a great idler. He appears in
lonely valleys, always with a pipe in his
mouth, and spends his time in making
love to shepherdesses and milkmaids.

4. *The Far Darrig* (Ir. *Fear Dearg,
i.e.* red man).—This is the practical joker
of the other world. The wild Sligo story
I give of 'A Fairy Enchantment' was
probably his work. Of these solitary
and mainly evil fairies there is no more
lubberly wretch than this same Far
Darrig. Like the next phantom, he pre-
sides over evil dreams.

5. *The Pooka* (Ir. *Púca,* a word
derived by some from *poc,* a he-goat).—
The Pooka seems of the family of the
nightmare. He has most likely never
appeared in human form, the one or two
recorded instances being probably mis-
takes, he being mixed up with the Far
Darrig. His shape is usually that of a
horse, a bull, a goat, eagle, or ass. His
delight is to get a rider, whom he rushes
with through ditches and rivers and
over mountains, and shakes off in the

gray of the morning. Especially does he love to plague a drunkard : a drunkard's sleep is his kingdom. At times he takes more unexpected forms than those of beast or bird. The one that haunts the Dun of Coch-na-Phuca in Kilkenny takes the form of a fleece of wool, and at night rolls out into the surrounding fields, making a buzzing noise that so terrifies the cattle that unbroken colts will run to the nearest man and lay their heads upon his shoulder for protection.

6. *The Dullahan.*—This is a most gruesome thing. He has no head, or carries it under his arm. Often he is seen driving a black coach called coach-a-bower (Ir. *Coite-bodhar*), drawn by headless horses. It rumbles to your door, and if you open it a basin of blood is thrown in your face. It is an omen of death to the houses where it pauses. Such a coach not very long ago went through Sligo in the gray of the morning, as was told me by a sailor who believed he saw it. In one village I know its rumbling is said to be heard many times in the year.

7. *The Leanhaun Shee* (Ir. *Lean-haun sidhe, i.e.* fairy mistress).—This spirit seeks the love of men. If they refuse, she is their slave; if they consent, they are hers, and can only escape by finding one to take their place. Her lovers waste away, for she lives on their life. Most of the Gaelic poets, down to quite recent times, have had a Leanhaun Shee, for she gives inspiration to her slaves and is indeed the Gaelic muse—this malignant fairy. Her lovers, the Gaelic poets, died young. She grew restless, and carried them away to other worlds, for death does not destroy her power.

8. *The Far Gorta* (man of hunger). —This is an emaciated fairy that goes through the land in famine time, begging and bringing good luck to the giver.

9. *The Banshee* (Ir. *Bean-sidhe, i.e.* fairy woman).—This fairy, like the Far Gorta, differs from the general run of solitary fairies by its generally good disposition. She is perhaps not really one of them at all, but a sociable fairy grown solitary through much sorrow.

The name corresponds to the less common Far Shee (Ir. *Fear Sidhe*), a man fairy. She wails, as most people know, over the death of a member of some old Irish family. Sometimes she is an enemy of the house and screams with triumph, but more often a friend. When more than one Banshee comes to cry, the man or woman who is dying must have been very holy or very brave. Occasionally she is most undoubtedly one of the sociable fairies. Cleena, once an Irish princess and then a Munster goddess, and now a Sheoque, is thus mentioned by the greatest of Irish antiquarians.

O'Donovan, writing in 1849 to a friend, who quotes his words in the *Dublin University Magazine*, says : 'When my grandfather died in · Leinster in 1798, Cleena came all the way from Ton Cleena to lament him ; but she has not been heard ever since lamenting any of our race, though I believe she still weeps in the mountains of Drumaleaque in her own country, where so many of the race of Eoghan More are dying of starvation.' The Banshee on the other hand who cries

with triumph is often believed to be no
fairy but a ghost of one wronged by an
ancestor of the dying. Some say wrongly
that she never goes beyond the seas,
but dwells always in her own country.
Upon the other hand, a distinguished
writer on anthropology assures me that
he has heard her on 1st December 1867,
in Pital, near Libertad, Central America,
as he rode through a deep forest. She
was dressed in pale yellow, and raised a
cry like the cry of a bat. She came to
announce the death of his father. This
is her cry, written down by him with the
help of a Frenchman and a violin.

He saw and heard her again on 5th
February 1871, at 16 Devonshire Street,
Queen's Square, London. She came this
time to announce the death of his eldest
child; and in 1884 he again saw and heard
her at 28 East Street, Queen's Square,
the death of his mother being the cause.

The Banshee is called *badh* or *bowa*

in East Munster, and is named *Bachuntha* by Banim in one of his novels.

Other Fairies and Spirits.—Besides the foregoing, we have other solitary fairies, of which too little definite is known to give them each a separate mention. They are the House Spirits, of whom 'Teigue of the Lee' is probably an instance ; the Water Sherie, a kind of will-o'-the-wisp ; the Sowlth, a formless luminous creature ; the Pastha (*Piast-bestia*), the lake dragon, a guardian of hidden treasure ; and the Bo men fairies, who live in the marshes of County Down and destroy the unwary. They may be driven away by a blow from a particular kind of sea-weed. I suspect them of being Scotch fairies imported by Scotch settlers. Then there is the great tribe of ghosts called Thivishes in some parts.

These are all the fairies and spirits I have come across in Irish folklore. There are probably many others undiscovered.

W. B. YEATS.

Co. DOWN, *June* 1891.

AUTHORITIES ON IRISH FOLKLORE

CROKER'S *Legends of the South of Ireland* ; Lady Wilde's *Ancient Legends of Ireland*, and *Ancient Charms* ; Sir William Wilde's *Irish Popular Superstitions* ; McAnally's *Irish Wonders* ; *Irish Folklore*, by Lageniensis (Father O'Hanlan) ; Curtins's *Myths and Folklore of Ireland*; Douglas Hyde's *Beside the Fire* and his *Leabhar Sgeulaigheachta* ; Patrick Kennedy's *Legendary Fictions of the Irish Peasantry*, his *Banks of the Boro*, his *Evenings on the Duffrey*, and his *Legends of Mount Leinster*; the chapbooks, *Royal Fairy Tales*, and *Tales of the Fairies*. There is also much folklore in Carleton's *Traits and Stories* ;

in Lover's *Legends and Stories of the Irish Peasantry*; in Mr. and Mrs. S. C. Hall's *Ireland*; in Lady Chatterton's *Rambles in the South of Ireland*; in Gerald Griffen's *Tales of a Jury Room* in particular, and in his other books in general. It would repay the trouble if some Irish magazine would select from his works the stray legends and scraps of fairy belief. There is much in the *Collegians*. There is also folklore in the chap-book *Hibernian Tales*, and a Banshee story or two will be found in Miss Lefanu's *Memoirs of my Grandmother*, and in Barrington's *Recollections*. There are also stories in Donovan's introduction to the *Four Masters*. The best articles are those in the *Dublin and London Magazine* (" The Fairy Greyhound " is from this collection) for 1827 and 1829, about a dozen in all, and David Fitzgerald's various contributions to the *Review Celtique* in our own day, and Miss M'Clintock's articles in the *Dublin University Magazine* for 1878. There are good articles also in the *Dublin University Magazine* for 1839, and much Irish folklore is within the pages of the *Folklore Journal* and the *Folklore Record*, and in the proceedings of the *Kilkenny Archæological Society*. The *Penny Journal*, the *Newry Magazine*, *Duffy's Sixpenny Magazine*, and the *Hibernian Magazine*, are also worth a search by any Irish writer on the look-out for subjects for song or ballad. My own articles in the *Scots Observer* and *National Observer* give many gatherings from the little-reaped Connaught fields. I repeat this list of authorities from my *Fairy and Folk Tales of the Irish Peasantry*,—a compilation from some of the sources mentioned,—bringing it down to date and making one or two corrections. The reader who would know Irish tradition should read these books above all others—Lady Wilde's *Ancient Legends*, Douglas Hyde's *Beside the Fire*, and a book not mentioned in the foregoing list, for it deals with the bardic rather than the folk literature, Standish O'Grady's *History of Ireland, Heroic Period*—perhaps the most imaginative book written on any Irish subject in recent decades.

A

SELECTED LIST

OF

JUVENILE BOOKS

— ✳ —

Crown 8vo, cloth, 5s.

CHILDREN'S STORIES IN ENG-LISH LITERATURE, from Shakespeare to Tennyson. By H. C. WRIGHT.

"A genial book."—*Speaker.*

— ✳ —

Crown 8vo, cloth, gilt edges, 5s.

BOYS' OWN STORIES. By ASCOTT R. HOPE. 3rd Edition. Eight Illustrations.

"The stories are well told."—*Pall Mall Gazette.*

I

Crown 8vo, cloth, gilt edges, 5s.

ROYAL YOUTHS: A Book of Princehoods. By ASCOTT R. HOPE. Illustrated.

"Well told and full of interest."—*National Observer.*

— ✳ —

Large crown 8vo, cloth, gilt edges, 5s.

ROBINSON CRUSOE. Newly Edited after the original Editions. 19 full-page Illustrations.

"Gives an account of Defoe which is very much to the point."—*Spectator.*

— ✳ —

Imperial 16mo, cloth extra, gilt edges, 3s. 6d.

DICK'S HOLIDAYS, and What He Did with Them. Illustrated. Cheaper Edition.

"A volume for which every budding botanist who gets it has good reason to be thankful."—*Pall Mall Gazette.*

— ✳ —

Small 8vo, cloth, gilt edges, 3s. 6d.

WHEN MOTHER WAS LITTLE. By S. P. YORKE. 13 full-page Illustrations,

"In all respects an agreeable and well-written story."—*Spectator.*

8vo, cloth, gilt edges, 6s.

TWO LITTLE CONFEDERATES.

By THOMAS NELSON PAGE. Illustrated.

"A delightful book."—*Saturday Review.*

—✻—

Medium 4to, paper boards, 3s. 6d.

DADDY JAKE, the Runaway, and

Other Stories. By JOEL CHANDLER HARRIS
(" Uncle Remus "). Illustrated.

"A fresh and delightful addition to those quaint and
laughable tales which have made the author of ' Uncle
Remus ' loved and fancied wherever the English tongue
is spoken."—*Observer.*

—✻—

Crown 8vo, cloth, 5s.

SIX GIRLS: A Home Story. By

FANNIE B. IRVING. Illustrated.

"Its interest is well sustained from first to last."—
Scotsman.

—✻—

Square Imperial 16mo, cloth, 5s.

IN THE TIME OF ROSES: A

Tale of Two Summers. By FLORENCE
SCANNELL. 32 Illustrations.

"A very successful book."—*Academy.*

Crown 8vo, cloth gilt, bevelled boards, 3s. 6d.

ALEXIS AND HIS FLOWERS. By

BEATRIX CRESSWELL. Illustrated.

"The book is a very pleasant one—a nosegay of everlasting blooms of fancy."—*Academy.*

——✶——

Square 8vo, cloth, 3s. 6d.

THE PRINCE OF THE HUNDRED

SOUPS. By VERNON LEE. Illustrated.

"I devoured it from cover to cover with a new zest."
—*Truth.*

——✶——

Imperial 16mo, cloth, 3s. 6d.

THE BIRD'S NEST, and Other Ser-

mons for Children of all ages. By Rev. S. Cox, D.D. 3rd Edition.

"Real honest preaching made fascinating and in-structive by an exquisite literary style."—*Methodist Times.*

——✶——

Small crown 8vo, cloth, 2s. 6d.

EVERY-DAY MIRACLES. By BED-

FORD POLLARD. Illustrated.

"A work worthy of the highest praise."—*Graphic.*

——✶——

Imperial 16mo, cloth gilt, gilt edges, 3s. 6d.

FAIRY TALES FROM BRENTANO.

Told in English by KATE F. KRŒKER. 3rd Edition.

"Welcome in the nursery. The translation has been very cleverly accomplished."—*Academy.*

Illustrated paper boards, 5s. ; cloth, gilt edges, 6s.

NEW FAIRY TALES FROM BRENTANO. By KATE F. KRŒKER. 8 coloured Illustrations.

"I read the book with edification and delight."—*Truth.*

— ✳ —

Medium 4to, paper boards, 3s. 6d.

THE BROWNIES : Their Book. By PALMER COX. 4th Edition. Illustrated.

"The Brownies are such prime favourites."—*Guardian.*

— ✳ —

Medium 4to, cloth, 6s.

ANOTHER BROWNIE BOOK. By PALMER COX. Illustrated.

"The illustrations are perhaps even more mirthful than the letterpress, but both are admirable."—*Morning Post.*

— ✳ —

4to, bevelled boards, 3s. 6d.

MARJORIE AND HER PAPA : How they wrote a Story and made Pictures for it. A Book for Children.

"Altogether a book to be desired by and for children."—*Spectator.*

THE

"LIVES WORTH LIVING" SERIES

OF

POPULAR BIOGRAPHIES

◆◆◆

Illustrated, crown 8vo, cloth,
price 3s. 6d. each.

1. LEADERS OF MEN. By H. A.
PAGE.

"Vigorously and well executed."—*Literary Churchman.*

2. WISE WORDS AND LOVING
DEEDS. By E. CONDER GRAY.

"The book is altogether a bracing one."—*Hand and Heart.*

3. MASTER MISSIONARIES. By
A. H. JAPP.

"The sketches are ably written."—*Glasgow Herald.*

4. LABOUR AND VICTORY. By A.
H. JAPP.

"Charming sketches."—*Glasgow Mail.*

5. HEROIC ADVENTURE : Exploration and Discovery.

"The book is one we can thoroughly recommend."
Christian.

6. GREAT MINDS IN ART.   By
   WILLIAM TIREBUCK.

   "Told with accuracy and freshness."—*Globe.*

7. GOOD MEN AND TRUE.   By
   ALEX. H. JAPP.

   "Valuable and interesting records."—*Freeman.*

8. THE LIVES OF ROBERT AND
   MARY MOFFAT.   By their Son, JOHN
   SMITH MOFFAT.

   "Eminently deserving of a permanent record.   Mr.
   Moffat's work is calculated to increase the veneration
   with which the memory of the veteran missionary is
   regarded by multitudes."—*Athenæum.*

9. FAMOUS   MUSICAL   COM-
   POSERS.   By LYDIA J. MORRIS.

   "Makes a capital gift-book."—*Scotsman.*

Printed by R. & R. CLARK, *Edinburgh*